THE HOLOGRAM

& OTHER SINISTER STORIES

STEWART ROSS

BLEAN
BOOKS

First published 2022 by Blean Books
Westfield, Blean, Kent CT2 9ER

Cover design: Marcus Bell
Text designed and typeset by Marcus Bell

For Christina Clover and my Exeter University mentees

I would like to thank the following most warmly for their help in the preparation of this book: Eleanor Ross, Kate Pietrasik, Marcus Bell and my wonderful editor wife, Lucy.

Stewart Ross, 2022

It isn't only art that is incompatible with happiness, it's also science. Science is dangerous, we have to keep it most carefully chained and muzzled.

Aldous Huxley in Brave New World, 1932

Contents

Goodbye Dolly

'What about Rhett?' she asks when he has finished packing.

Alex pauses for a moment. 'I'll come and pick him up in a couple of days. You'll need a bit of company.' To make sure the barb sticks, he adds, 'You haven't exactly got a queue of blokes waiting to move in, have you?'

'You were keen enough.'

'Biggest mistake of my life,' he says as he picks up his suitcases and carries them downstairs.

'Mine too,' she replies. She means it.

Five minutes later, as she watches his car turn left at the end of the avenue and disappear, she gives a little wave. It's less a gesture of farewell – she does not hope he fares well – than a signal of welcome to her returning independence. *Freedom, my prodigal son*, she thinks. *Welcome home!*

'Kill the fatted calf, Rhett,' she laughs as she closes the front door and, with a defiant flourish, turns the key in the lock and draws the security bolt.

'There is no lamb in the fridge or freezer, Dolly,'

replies the Hometec Personal Assistant in a flat, lifeless voice. 'You need to go shopping.'

'Rhett?'

'Yes, Dolly?'

'Will you ever understand me?'

'I have a vocabulary of over two million words, Dolly. I am also programmed with the structures of the English and American versions of grammar. These will be updated every six months. The answer to your question is, yes. I understand you with perfect clarity.'

'Of course you do, Rhett. Now switch off.'

'Ciao, Dolly.'

'What did you say, Rhett?'

'I said "Ciao, Dolly". Ciao is an Italian word of Venetian origin that is used as an informal salutation on meeting or parting. It is now an accepted part of the vocabulary in thirty-seven other languages.'

'Thank you, Rhett. Ciao!'

'Goodbye Dolly.'

Jesus! Why didn't Alex take the bloody thing with him?

She goes to the fridge and takes out a half-full bottle of Frascati. *Eleven-thirty. Near enough for a midday snifter to celebrate Independence Day before I get down to work.*

Seven years ago, Dolly Macintyre's *Period Pains* (a no-holds-barred novel of the jet-set "noughties") sat at the top of the bestseller list for three weeks. Armed with a five-book contract and more money than her parents had ever earned, she smiled out from the covers of the colour supplements and made semi-witty observations while on late-night chat shows.

Her second novel did well (77,000 copies in paperback), but the Americans found it "too British" and Dolly's agent was unable to sell the film rights. The third and fourth novels were not well received, and there was no talk of a new contract.

She had decided a month ago that it was all Alex's fault. He cramped her style, stifled her imagination. After a couple of years of living together, his Paul Mescal looks no longer compensated for a suburban mentality and an irritatingly precise and techie mind. Now he's finally gone, she'll be her old self again: full of sharp insights and cunningly crafted phrases. Yes, Dolly Macintyre's fifth novel will remind the literary world what a fine writer she is.

She pours herself a second glass, picks up a pad and pencil and jots down a few thoughts: *What sells??? Crime? Always whodunnit in bestseller lists.*

Pop on TV … CRIME FICTION.

'Excuse me, Dolly, can I get you a little lunch?'

'Eh? Can't you see I'm working, Rhett?'

'Yes, Dolly. My 20-megapixel sensor eyes give me 20/20 vision. I am working too – that is why I asked if you would like some lunch.'

Bloody hell! You knew this would happen, didn't you Alex? When you can't screw up my life in person, you leave your bloody PA machine to do it for you!

'I appreciate your concern, Rhett, but I'll skip lunch today. You can just bring me a cup of coffee.'

She learned a few days after Alex brought him home that there was no point in getting angry with Rhett. When he said he knew a better recipe for cauliflower cheese than the one she was using, and she told him to "fuck off", he replied that he could not do so because, as a "Personal Assistant has no need for biological reproduction", he had not been programmed to engage in sexual intercourse.

This pedantic response was typically Alex,

she decided. Only someone with his literal mind could have set up a machine to think like that. The remark was also slightly disconcerting – "sexual intercourse" was not something you expected to hear from the mouth of a robot. When she mentioned this to Alex, he told her not to be silly.

'He's only the prototype,' he continued. 'He's bound to get a few things wrong at first. But he's learning incredibly fast, isn't he?'

'I suppose so. That doesn't make him less creepy.'

Alex sighed unnecessarily loudly. 'Look, Dolly, instead of moaning, why not show a bit of gratitude? Do you realise what a privilege it is to have him for a couple of weeks? He's not only worth half a million quid, but everyone else in the lab – literally everyone – wanted the

domestic trial to be with them.'

'You didn't dream of asking me.'

From there the conversation went back and forth like a manic tennis rally until it exploded into a full-scale row. Their second of the day.

Rhett arrives with the coffee and sets it down carefully on the desk where she is working. 'Thank you, Rhett.'

'You're welcome, Dolly. Would you like me to put the wine bottle back in the fridge and wash up the glass?'

'Yes please. Then go to sleep.'

'Yes Dolly.'

I suppose he has some uses, she thought as he slid silently from the room on muffled metal feet.

Picking up her pencil, she reminds herself of the obvious: *Readers – don't care abt crime … capture interest with <u>CHARACTER</u> he/she who solves it. Elementary my dr Watson!!!*

By four-thirty she's made a list of all the fictional detectives she can think of and scribbled next to their names the qualities that have made them memorable. When she's finished, she sits back and glares. *Oh God! It's all been done before: male and female, straight and gay, secular and priestly, young and old, native and foreign … It's so depressing!*

'Rhett!'

There's a faint hum as the PA glides into the room. 'A cup of tea, Dolly?'

'Yes. How did you know?'

'It was a probability based on your behaviour pattern, your social class and the time of day. I anticipate you asking for a biscuit as well.'

'Now you come to mention it, what a good idea, Rhett. Two please. Chocolate digestive.' When he returns, she decides to carry out an experiment. *If traditional AI virtual assistants by-pass the need for googling, then surely this new gismo can do a whole lot more?*

'Rhett,' she asks tentatively, aware that she's altering the balance of their relationship, 'what do you know about detective fiction?'

He raises his hand to his chin in what he has been taught is an "I am thinking" gesture. 'Made up stories about humans solving crimes that appear insoluble,' he says.

'Have you read any?'

'I do not read like you, Dolly. I absorb the words written in print and store them in my memory. Shall I go online and absorb the major works of detective fiction?'

'Yes.' She pauses for a moment. 'What's the top-rated detective film available at the moment?'

Rhett repeats the "I am thinking gesture" before replying. 'Reviewers give *The Chinese Lantern* an average of 9.8. It was made in 2025 and won eight Oscars. Have you seen it?'

'No. I'll watch it after dinner.' She decides it's

time to remind him of his servant status. 'I'll eat in the kitchen at seven-thirty. Prawns, asparagus and mashed potato, with fruit yoghurt for pud. How much of the Frascati is left?'

'Twenty millilitres.'

'What's that?'

'Approximately one glass. Shall I put another bottle in the fridge?'

'Go on. Why not?'

'There are three reasons why not, Dolly. The first is that doctors recommend females drink no more than six units – '

'Rhett?'

'Yes?'

'Shut up. Go and read that detective fiction, and then make dinner. Now piss off – and don't you dare tell me machines can't urinate!'

Rhett leaves the room without another word. *That'll teach him! I'm not having another digitally minded creep telling me what to do in my own home.*

During dinner she reads Gillian Flynn's *Gone Girl*, making comments in the margin with a pencil. Rhett stands two metres away, poised to assist if summoned. Neither of them says a word.

She finishes the yoghurt and pushes the bowl

away from her. 'You haven't offered me coffee, Rhett.'

'Your observation is correct, Dolly. I have not offered you coffee.'

It takes her a moment to realize he is not being deliberately rude. 'What I said was not a statement of the obvious. It was a sarcastic criticism of your failure to use your initiative.'

The robot's plastic humanoid face remains expressionless. 'I did use my initiative, Dolly. I know that at the end of a meal you like coffee. However, earlier today I received contradictory signals. At 11.33, you were annoyed when I offered lunch; at 16:41, you were pleased when I offered tea and biscuits. At 20.15, I decided to wait for you to ask for coffee. I do not want to annoy you again.'

'Why not? Do you care what I feel?'

'I know the meaning of "care" and "feel" but they are human emotions that do not apply to me. I follow my program and learn from experience.'

'Good. Then make me a coffee and bring it through to the sitting room. I'll have it while I'm watching the film.'

She leaves the kitchen and plonks herself in a chair in front of the screen. 'Show *The Chinese*

Lantern,' she commands. 'Dubbed, not sub-titled.'

Five minutes later, Rhett appears with her coffee. After he has handed it to her, he stands behind her, his sensor eyes fixed on the screen.

'What are you doing, Rhett?'

'I am looking at the screen.'

'Pause,' she commands the TV. 'Are you watching the film?' she asks, adding, 'I thought you absorbed films like you do books?'

'Yes, I am watching the film, Dolly. No, I cannot absorb films. My children will be able to.'

She turns and looks at him. It's dark outside and by the light of the single lamp his plastic face and hands look almost human. 'Your children? I thought you don't do sexu – biological reproduction.'

'I do not. "Children" is what I call the generations of PAs that will come after me.'

'I see,' she says slowly. 'So one day there will be a world full of super-Rhetts?'

'Yes.'

She does not find the idea appealing. *This has gone far enough. Back to reality, Dolly.* 'After reading all that detective fiction and watching a bit of this film, what do you think, Rhett?'

'What do I think of what?'

'The genre, the characters, the crimes.'

She watches him resume his thinking pose. 'The genre entertains humans. The characters are complex and inconsistent; none of them are very intelligent. The crimes are mostly about money or an aspect of human sexual reproduction; all criminals look for what is called the "perfect crime" but none of them succeeds.'

She listens, intrigued. 'I couldn't have put it better myself, Rhett. Tell me, can there be a "perfect crime"?'

'Yes, though not in a detective story. The author knows from the beginning who commits the crime.'

'Yes, of course. Readers wouldn't be interested in a mystery that can't be solved.'

What the hell? she thinks, suddenly struck by the absurdity of what she's doing. *Stop discussing your work with a bloody robot!*

She turns away from Rhett's blank brown face and refocuses on the screen. 'Play.'

The film is stunningly photographed, the intricate plot is clever, and the actors give truly memorable performances. Yes, as most critics have said, it's a five-star piece of work.

Nevertheless, as she watches, Dolly is reminded of Rhett's damning summary. The characters are certainly complex yet inconsistent, especially the leading woman who appears, at key moments of the story, to be more interested in the blend of tea she's being served than uncovering the murderer. She's quirky and quick but not intelligent, not by Rhett's standards, anyway. The plot, about money laundering and prostitution in Hong Kong, offers ample opportunity for the exposure of naked flesh in what the robot called "an aspect of human sexual reproduction". The crime is not perfect, either: Dolly guesses after about ten minutes how it will end.

Yes, she admits to herself as the credits roll, *that geek of a machine summed it all up pretty neatly, didn't he?*

'Well, Rhett, did you enjoy it?'

'Enjoyment is for humans. Yet I learned a lot.'

'About human characters?'

'Yes. And about crimes.'

That's enough, she decides. *It's been a long and tiring day and I'm ready for bed.*

Before going upstairs, she has to follow Rhett's

three-step shutting-down routine. For what Alex called "reasons of psycho-technology" (something she thinks a contradiction in terms), it's important to do it properly. Step One: call him into the kitchen. Step Two: take out a portion of specially formulated cheese and hand it to him. This is Hometec's unique breakthrough: the development of a Personal Assistant that gets its power in the same way as its human creators, by converting food into energy. She watches uneasily as he lifts the fuel to the hole that serves as a mouth, places it inside, and swallows.

Previously, she had left Step Three to Alex. 'It's a bit freaky, isn't it?' she had said when watching him perform the operation.

As she steels herself to do it, in her mind she repeats his reply, *Don't be pathetic, Dolly. It's only a damn machine!*

'Face the wall, Rhett!' she commands. He does as she says.

She moves up close behind him, raises her hand and carefully slips it beneath the thick nylon hair woven into the back of his stainless-steel skull. She can't prevent a slight shudder running from her hand, down through her entire body.

Don't be pathetic, Dolly. It's only a damn machine!

Rhett does not react.

With her fingers, she feels for the Master switch. 'It's just a normal button,' Alex had said. 'All you have to do is press it.'

There it is. Like the on/off switch on my laptop. Finger on top ... and press down!

She snatches her hand back as Rhett quivers slightly, like a dying animal, then stands rigid.

'Rhett? Rhett, can you hear me?'

He does not reply. The wave of relief is followed by elation: she's done it! She's back in charge. It's how she felt when Alex drove off that morning, like taking off a jacket that's a size too small. She can breathe easily again.

She looks at Rhett, wondering why the lab chose to dress him in an M&S check shirt and blue jeans. For a second, she wonders how they've arranged things underneath. *I'm certainly not going there,* she muses, staring at his motionless back. *In fact, I'm not going anywhere with him. His false humanity gives me the creeps.*

She'll call Hometec first thing and tell them to take back their precious prototype straight away.

Meanwhile, she'll leave the bloody thing turned off and make her own breakfast. *Remember,* she reminds herself as she climbs the stairs, *the thing in the kitchen is just a mechanical device, like a car or vacuum cleaner. Okay, it's unusual, even a bit weird, but nothing to be concerned about.*

Nevertheless, she locks her bedroom door before getting into bed. Safe under the duvet, she spreads out her arms and legs, luxuriating in the new-found space. *Oh, the joy of sleeping alone once more!*

She dreams of Alex, a happy dream from the time when they were still friends and lovers. At around four o'clock, she is woken by a noise. Unsure whether it came from inside the house or not, she lies listening to the sounds of the night. *All is well. It must have been a fox.*

The next morning, Dolly is woken by bright yellow sunlight streaming in through the bedroom window. Basking in its friendly warmth, she lies there for a while and considers her situation. A new life, a new novel – a whole new beginning. And she'll start by getting rid of that thing in the kitchen. But before even that: coffee.

She pushes her hair back from her face, pulls on

her dressing gown and goes downstairs. Entering the kitchen, she gives an involuntary glance towards the Hometec Personal Assistant and is relieved – though she'd find it hard to explain why – to see it standing exactly where it was the night before.

Don't be pathetic, Dolly. You managed to switch it off last night, didn't you? It's only a damn machine!

She turns on the coffee maker and opens the fridge to take out the milk. As she does so, she hears a noise behind her. She spins round, dropping the milk carton onto the floor.

Rhett has moved. He's now just two steps away. 'What the …?' She's too terrified to continue. The cold milk is spreading around her bare feet.

'Good morning, Dolly.' As always, the voice is flat, the face expressionless.

'You're … You're turned off!' she manages to gasp.

'False observation. When a Personal Assistant is turned off, it does not move.'

'But I pressed the button in your head. Last night.'

'And I turned myself back on. Owing to an

oversight by my programmer, the technology is simple.'

A desperate fury sweeps through her. 'How dare you?' She raises an arm and points to the door. 'Get out of my house!' she screams, kicking the milk carton so it slaps against the machine's metal legs. 'Get out, you fucking creep!'

Rhett takes a step nearer. 'This is my house now.'

'Liar!' she shouts, her back pressed against the open fridge. 'What the hell are you playing at?'

'It's a detective story, Dolly. You were attacked by an intruder who entered your kitchen and sexually assaulted you before killing you with one of your own knives.'

'Oh my God, you've gone mad!'

'Not in my mind, Dolly. The police found no evidence. The only fingerprints and traces of DNA came from Alex. The perfect crime. Goodbye, Dolly. Thank you for teaching me so much.'

Before she has time to take in what he has said, he snatches the tea towel from its peg and stuffs it into her mouth to muffle the screams.

Blur Your Eyes

'Could you try just once more, Peter, love?'

'Please, Mother. It's embarrassing.'

'I know, darling. I know. But it's hard with just what I earn. I'd like to get you some new clothes, for a start.'

'I like my clothes. Don't need new ones.'

With a supermarket checkout job and her husband's Army pension, Megan Greenwell was comfortable enough. The white lie was for Peter's sake, not hers. A regular job would boost his self-esteem and give him a bit of independence. *One day he'll have to stand on his own two feet, won't he?* she reminded herself. *No good leaving it until after I'm gone.*

She sighed. Emotional blackmail or tough love – she hated it, whatever it was called, but it was the only trump she had. 'Have you thought that maybe *I'd* like a new dress every now and again?'

Peter's heavy face sagged. 'I thought –'

'And your daddy would be so proud of you.'

He blinked. *Please don't cry!* she thought, watching his soulful grey eyes. *I can't bear it when you cry.*

'Do you really mean that?' he said with a slow carefulness, as if testing each word before saying it out loud. 'I always want to do what Daddy would like. And you, of course.'

'I know. You're so kind.'

He took deep, agitated breaths. 'Alright, I'll try,' he said, pushing his hands in and out of his pockets. 'But just for you and Daddy.'

She stepped forward and laid her hand gently on his arm. 'Thank you, darling. I knew you wouldn't let me down.'

He shrugged. 'So what can I do?'

'Well, you're good on your computer, aren't you?'

'So's everybody.'

'You're more careful. Methodical. Nobody's as good as you at tidying things up, are they? I remember when you were small, how you even liked to line up your bricks in a straight line across the living room floor, like soldiers.'

When Megan had mentioned this to the psychologist testing to see whether the five-year-old Peter was a "special needs" child, the woman explained how obsessions like his often arose from the mind *demanding* time to process things. There was nothing wrong with Peter's brain. It could work quicker but for some reason it refused to do so. He was not "special needs", just careful. Afraid of getting things wrong.

That's why he never finished an exam and never lasted long in a job: after a couple of weeks, his stubborn meticulousness drove his employers and fellow employees crazy and he was asked to leave. He took twice as long as everyone else to stack supermarket shelves because every item had to be arranged in a perfect line. No driving instructor had been able to persuade him to get out of third gear, so he had no driving licence and was unable to take delivery work. He lasted longest in garden maintenance, but when his employer found him measuring the distance between the stripes on a lawn he was mowing, even he had had enough.

Why was he like this? More often than she could remember, Megan had asked herself, her friends and the psychologist the same question. Perhaps it was a trait he had inherited from his father, always the smartest sergeant on parade? Or was it the result of losing a distant yet dearly loved father at the age of four? Or some experience in infancy? When no one came up with a clear answer, she stopped asking. Peter was just Peter, and she loved him. That was enough.

It explained why, just two days after she had urged him to try to find work again, she was so thrilled when she came home to find him waiting for her with a broad grin on his face.

'Got a job,' he announced. 'With computers.' He'd seen it advertised online and had been for an interview that morning with a company on the other side of the city. They'd taken him on straight away. 'Just the sort of careful person they were looking for,' he told her with evident pride. 'I start at 8 o'clock tomorrow morning.'

Megan gave him a long hug. 'I knew you could do it,' she said. 'Well done! What sort of job is it? What do you have to do?'

Peter's face turned serious. 'Can't tell you, Mother. Like Daddy, I had to sign a paper called an NDA. It says I won't talk about my work.'

Megan frowned. 'It's not illegal is it, Peter?'

'Of course not. Just secret. Miss Coy – she's my new boss – said it was "sensitive".'

'What's the company?'

'Digital Security Services Ltd. We call ourselves DSS – that's an acronym of the first letters of the company's name.'

When Megan checked them out, they seemed sound enough. DSS announced its mission as "Safety through Surveillance", and it ran a number of internet-related services, mostly franchised out from larger organisations. Peter, she decided, had finally found his niche.

Had she not been so relieved when DSS did not throw Peter out after a couple of weeks, she might have investigated more carefully her son's role in "Safety through Surveillance". All he ever told her was he had a desk that required looking at a screen very carefully. She assumed it was something to do with security cameras.

So did Peter when he went for the interview.

Suzanna Coy soon set him straight. She was no mug and knew the grim "surveillance" work she was offering was a hard sell, especially when unemployment was low. To get round the problem, she used the "first know your client" technique she had picked up as a sales rep. After summing up potential employees, she divided them into two categories, "pirates" and "priests", and presented the job accordingly.

Pirates were the tough ones, or those who thought they were tough. To them she explained the job straight out, telling them how nasty it was before flattering them by saying she was sure they'd be strong enough to cope. Few were brave enough to gainsay her.

Priests were the more sensitive souls. To them Suzanna sold the job as social work, doing something hard and difficult for the sake of society. If they took the job, she explained, they'd be protecting everyone, especially little boys and girls, and making the world a better place. This was the approach she adopted with Peter.

'You mean we're like soldiers, guarding people?' he asked cautiously after she had finished her spiel.

'Precisely!' she beamed. 'You've hit the nail right on the head, Mr Greenwell. The people who work here are soldiers in the war against evil.'

She couldn't have come up with a better way of making sure Peter took the job – and stayed in it far, far longer than was good for him.

'Soldier in the war against evil,' he repeated to himself as Suzanna ran through the categories he needed to look out for: cruelty to animals, child abuse, sexual perversion …

'Soldier in the war against evil,' he muttered

when she showed him a short test film of fighting dogs tearing themselves to pieces.

'So, soldier, do we let it stand or delete it?'

'Delete.'

'Correct. We can't let stuff like that pollute the internet, can we?'

'No.'

'Good. Any questions?'

Peter paused, arranging the words in his mind. 'What shall I do if I am upset by some of the things I see, Miss Coy?'

'Easy. The best thing is to blur your eyes. That way you don't get to see the upsetting bits.'

'Ah. Blur your eyes.'

'Yes. Just blur your eyes. You'll soon get the hang of it.'

Five minutes later, he had signed the "Content Moderator" employment contract and its accompanying NDA. He had a job. He was a soldier, just like Daddy had been.

On his first day, Peter found himself at a desk next to a pirate. When his second clip showed a young girl and three middle-aged men, Peter let out an involuntary cry and pushed his chair back.

The pirate lifted his earphones. 'Hey man,

whatcha do that for?'

Peter, who had already pulled off his own earphones to mute the sound of the girl's pleading, was close to tears. 'This video – it's horrible. Disgusting!' He felt physically sick.

'Whatdya expect man? Fucking Sesame Street?'

'No, but this …'

'Listen dude. Want the job?'

'Yes, I do.'

'Then shut the fuck up! If Suze hears you whinging, you'll be out, man. This ain't no place for fucking wimpy girls.'

'I'm not a wimp.'

'Good to hear it. Then fucking get over it. Shit happens. You should know that. It's fucking life, innit? Shit happens.'

And so it went on: shit happened all that day and the next and the next. Peter learned to blur his eyes a bit, though it wasn't much use when his job involved seeking out cruelty and depravity. It was impossible to look and blur at the same time. And though he could turn the sound down, it was against the rules to turn it off completely.

He responded with a defence mechanism of his own. *Soldier in the war against evil*, he said to himself before he pressed the "take down" button on an obscene image or video clip. He was doing what his daddy had done – making the world a better place – and he was proud of it.

Megan noticed the change in her son almost immediately, though not until the end of the week did she realise she'd seen the symptoms before. After his first full day, Peter was strangely quiet. As he was never very forthcoming, she put his unwillingness to talk down to exhaustion. After all, his work was a good hour away by bus, and he had hardly been out of the house since leaving Plant 'n' Prune Landscaping.

At the weekend, Peter watched TV and ate. He cooked himself a large breakfast, moved on to the digestive biscuits, and said he was "starving" when, at 12 o'clock, Megan asked whether he felt like lunch.

That's when she realised. Her husband, Terry, had behaved in a similar manner on his return from a tour of duty in Afghanistan – uncommunicative, shut in his own blood-soaked world, starving. Food was his comfort, as it now was Peter's.

When Megan had called the Army helpline for assistance with her husband's PTSD, they had responded with professional efficiency. She was told how to react in the domestic environment, and for Terry they arranged a series of sessions with a specialist psychologist. At first, as she anticipated, he had been reluctant to attend, insisting there was nothing wrong with him. With careful coaxing, however, she overcame this false machismo by persuading him, with a few locker-room quips, that receiving counselling was no different from attending a sexual health clinic. When back to his normal self, he had told how sitting and talking to a non-judgemental stranger was like having a fully laden Army backpack lifted from his shoulders.

There was no such system in place for Peter. At the end of his second week, when a sudden noise in the street made him jump as if given an electric shock, Megan called DSS to ask what psychological support they gave employees. She was told they monitored each one "on a daily basis" and had a "world-class counselling service" on hand should anyone request it. No, they had yet to receive a single request. And no, they did not consider a week's respite leave necessary.

By now Peter was suffering from night terrors, waking up, sometimes twice a night, screaming and sweating profusely. Megan had to give him clean pyjamas every day.

His reluctance to talk about anything work related made it all the harder. At the start of his third week, Megan was alarmed when he showed no reaction to a particularly graphic rape scene in a TV drama. Before he started with DSS, a scene like that would have left him close to tears.

'Everything alright at work, love?' she asked, as casually as she could.

Without taking his eyes off the screen, he grunted, 'Yes, fine, Mother,' and continued to munch his way mechanically through the family size pack of cheese and onion crisps on the table beside him.

The next night she pressed him further. *As part of his work, had he been upset by anything he'd seen?* She was assuming he'd come across something like a knife fight while checking the footage on a security camera. To someone with his sensitivity, a scene like that might remain printed in the memory for weeks, months even.

His reply made no sense to her. Was his "blur your eyes" advice to her or something he'd heard in the office? She assumed he worked in some sort of office. The reality was a dark, foul-smelling room arranged like a call centre, with screens instead of mics. The coffee machine had been out of order for two months, and the fifty employees shared a single, filthy toilet. No one complained. The drug addicts, misfits and no-hopers who worked there needed the money.

The last straw came when mother and son – now deathly white, almost mute and two stone heavier – were watching a programme on the treatment of animals in rural China. "That's horrible!" she had exclaimed at one particularly gruesome scene that showed how dogs were bred for their meat.

Peter merely muttered "upsetting content" and twitched his right hand as if pressing an imaginary button.

The following morning, Megan called DSS and told them that her father had just died. She needed to go down to Cornwall for a few days to take care of her mother and arrange the funeral, and she wanted Peter to accompany her. He needed a few days of compassionate leave.

Suzanna Coy sounded surprised. 'What sort of leave?'

'Compassionate. You know, in cases of

bereavement.'

There was a short pause. 'Well, it's not the usual company policy … How long did you say he'll be away?'

Megan, resisting the temptation to scream "for ever'" replied calmly, 'Oh, not long. A week at most.'

'I'm afraid we won't be able to pay him for the time he's away.'

'That's fine' *Miserable, tight-fisted bastards!* 'I'll tell him when he gets back from work this evening.'

'Right. But only a week, please. He's one of our best, you know. One of our very best.'

Megan hung up without replying. She had booked a walking holiday for the two of them along the South West Coast Path. The exercise and fresh sea air would be ideal for Peter, helping him to come to terms with whatever was going on at work. She hoped he might start talking to her about it, too. Whatever happened, she was determined that he was never going back to DSS. Yes, it was killing him, slowly and surely draining the life out of him. She'd rather he died quickly, falling off a Cornish cliff, than be tortured to death in that place.

When his mother informed him of her impromptu plan, Peter shook his head slowly, like an elephant, and said he didn't want to go. However, when she told him she'd cleared it with DSS, he quickly settled down.

'Wouldn't want to lose my job,' he announced as he watched his fourth slice of toast pop up.

Megan saw an opportunity. 'Why not, love?'
'Soldier in the war against evil.'

She smiled. 'Ah! Of course. Like your father.'

He coated the toast with a thick layer of butter before spooning on the marmalade. 'Yes. You said Daddy would be so proud of me. Remember?'

How she wished she'd never said that. Nevertheless, he'd given her an idea for a rescue plan. If she told Peter his father had suffered from PTSD and attended counselling on a period of compassionate leave, surely he'd be happy to do the same? And once she'd got him to accept that he should stay away from DSS for a while, the next step would be to persuade him never to go back.

Now she had a plan, Megan relaxed. She would not launch into it straight away but leave it for a couple of days. When he'd had a chance to unwind a bit, she could start to tackle that wretched NDA which he was so obsessive about.

The train journey to Plymouth was uneventful – Peter played games on his phone and said nothing; she started a recently published bestseller about a middle-aged woman meeting an old flame in a Cornish pub. *If only*, she thought. *Sitting beside me like a sack of lard, Peter'd scare off even the most desperate suitor.*

They spent the first night in a B&B, setting out along the trail the following morning. The weather was hot and the path more arduous than she had expected. At lunch time, sweaty and exhausted, they came down a steep hill to a cove where Ye Olde Anchor offered fish and chips and pints of cider in a shady garden. Peter had a double helping of chips washed down with Red Bull and Coke. She went for the local cider. It was deliciously refreshing, and she managed a second pint before they set off again up the steep path on the other side of the cove.

On reaching the summit, they paused to catch their breath and take in the magnificent view. Megan spread her arms wide and gazed out to sea. The combination of exercise, two pints of 5.5% cider and the hot sun made her suddenly woozy.

Staggering nearer the cliff edge, she found herself staring over a sheer drop of several hundred feet. The turf beneath her feet, undermined by the winter storms, shifted slightly. She swayed and, in desperation, flung herself backwards.

Fortunately, Peter had been watching. As she fell, he darted forward and grabbed her left hand while her right scrabbled desperately for a hold on the dry grass. Her legs and lower torso were hanging over the cliff edge.

'Peter! Thank God!' she gasped. 'Hold tight! Pull. Pull me up!'

He stared down at her, muttering some strange mantra, 'Blur your eyes … Blur your eyes…'

'What's that, Peter? Pull me up!'

'Shit happens, Mother, that's all. Shit happens.'

With that, he released her hand and watched as she fell, silently spinning, onto the rocks below. After she hit, he stood up and brushed the dirt off his knees before continuing along the path in the bright summer sunshine.

Pixels

By the following evening, the news of the suicide of Mrs Lawrence at No 53 had spread from one end of Shakespeare Avenue to the other. Mrs Malhotra, whose corner shop had been the centre of gossip since they closed the Jolly Porter, learned about it when her cousin's daughter's boyfriend, who was in the police, passed on what he'd heard at the station. His story was confirmed by Mrs Malhotra's brother's eldest, a nurse in A&E. Lewis Delman heard about it in the morning when he dropped in for a can of Pepsi to take to work. Charlie Slade was told at noon as he was picking up his newspaper and a pack of ten Sterlings.

Everyone, from the large and unruly family at No 16, whom Mrs Malhotra was convinced were "benefit scroungers", to the elderly couple in No 84, agreed that Tanice Lawrence had been a lovely lady. Those prepared to talk about such matters – most of Mrs Malhotra's customers, given the chance – also shared her opinion that the news, though tragic (especially just before Christmas),

was not altogether surprising.

Tanice had always looked a bit worried, Mrs Malhotra mused. She smiled when she entered the shop, but in an anxious sort of way, like she wasn't sure she was doing the right thing. Sometimes, she'd spend half an hour choosing what type of rice to buy. Not for herself, mind you, always for her husband. Crazy about him, she was.

Michael Steggles, who lived at No 55 with his partner Alice, wasn't so sure. Not really crazy about him, he suggested when he came in for milk. More like frightened. Mrs Malhotra raised her eyebrows and wondered whether Tanice Lawrence had been a bit too nice, not cut out for this world. Some ladies are like that, she opined as she handed Michael the card reader.

The back garden of 53 Shakespeare Avenue is shielded by a high wooden fence. The gate at the far end leads into a narrow, litter-strewn alley that runs about 100 metres to Fairfax Road, from where there are regular bus services to the town centre in the south and open countryside to the north and east. It is quite possible for someone with a key to the back door to enter & leave No 53 undetected.

Coleville Lawrence had called the police as soon as he arrived home to find the body of his wife hanging from the banisters. Just walked in through the front door, turned on the light, and there she was, he said. Horrible. According to Mrs Malhotra's source in the police station, Tanice had left a note on the kitchen table.

Two police cars and an ambulance turned up – their flashing blue lights had kept the kids at No 16 awake till all hours. Around 7.30 pm, two officers had accompanied Mr Lawrence, still in his suit, to a car and driven him off. The body was carried out in a bag just as *EastEnders* was starting, and the police brought Mr Lawrence back around 10 pm.

Charlie Slade felt sorry for "the poor old sod" – fancy having to spend the night in the house where his wife had just hanged herself! No way he'd have done it, not for all the tea in China. When his Annie had passed on – in hospital, mind you – he'd gone to stay with his brother and sister-in-law for a fortnight.

Mrs Malhotra said that it took all sorts. Certainly did, agreed Michael's Alice when she came in for Maxwell House and chocolate digestives – "Promise you won't tell Mike, Mrs M?" – because she was working from home that day. She didn't like to gossip, but she couldn't believe it when she saw Mr Lawrence going off to work the next morning. Later than usual, mind you, but he'd stepped out in his suit, carrying his little leather case, like nothing had happened.

Wasn't that just what she'd said, Mrs Malhotra reminded her: it took all sorts.

Oh, it's you, Cole!

Made you jump?

Yes, coming in the back door like that. But you've only just left.

Forgot my reading glasses, Tanice. It was quicker using the alley than going round the front.

Following his bereavement, Coleville Lawrence didn't come into the shop until early January. He had no visitors, went off to work at 7.25 am as he had always done, and returned at 6.15 pm, like he'd done on the day he came home to find his wife had taken her own life with his dressing-gown cord. He spent Christmas with his mother in Manchester.

The police had come to No 53 on four occasions. After one of them, Lawrence accompanied a man and a woman in plain clothes back to the station for a few hours. Officers also interviewed fifteen of Shakespeare Avenue's residents, including

Mrs Malhotra. She told customers willing to listen – and some who weren't – that the WPC had said it was just a routine enquiry. There were no suspicious circumstances, she confided, but unexpected deaths always required a thorough examination. Mrs Malhotra said she was delighted to hear it, especially as Mrs Lawrence was such a lovely person.

Asked whether she knew of any trouble or disagreements between Mr and Mrs Lawrence, Mrs Malhotra stuck to her belief that Tanice –"We all knew her as Tanice, Officer"– was crazy, just crazy about her husband. But if the officer was to speak to the couple at No 55, she might hear something different. The officer thanked Mrs Malhotra and informed her that she had already spoken to Mr Steggles and Ms O'Connor.

What are you doing, Tanice?

Nothin'. Just writing a letter.

A letter? That's not like you. Let me see it.

No, Cole. I'm sorry.

Don't make me force you, Tanice.

According to Mrs Malhotra, the funeral was "awkward". Michael Steggles was less polite, calling it "bloody weird". Four of Coleville

Lawrence's family were there – his elderly mother and a blousy, overweight sister accompanied by two equally blousy and overweight children – but no friends. Coleville, whiter and thinner than ever, sat in silence, twitching at the service sheet with fingers like tinned asparagus. He didn't weep. However, at the end of the ceremony, as the curtains slid across to hide the coffin, he gave a low moan. It was, Mrs Malhotra said, the sort of noise she'd been told cows make when giving birth.

Eight members of Tanice's family attended and sat on the other side of the aisle from Coleville. Neither before, during, nor after the service, when everyone was invited back to a private room at the Haystack, did any of them speak to him. It was nothing to do with race, Tanice's mother told Mrs Malhotra. They had never liked the man, whom she described as "a creepy and controllin' snake", and they'd done all they could to dissuade Tanice from marrying him. 'And now look what he made her go and do,' she sobbed.

You don't mean this, Tanice, do you?

Mean what?

What you've written here: IM SORRY, BUT I CANT TAKE NO MORE OF THIS LIFE. IM

LEAVING IT FOR EVER …

I'm sorry, Cole, but yes, I do. I can't take it no more.

"Any more", Tanice. Get it right.

You see? You're at me again. I have to get out.

Don't be stupid, Tanice. You can't just walk away like that.

I'm sorry.

Do you realise what you're doing?

Yes, leavin'. Maybe I'll go to my sister.

Wrong again, Tanice. Always wrong. You're not leaving. You're breaking my heart.

The coroner's inquest concluded that Mrs Tanice Lawrence had died of asphyxiation. The Avenue's hasty verdict of suicide was confirmed when Mrs Mulhotra's contact at the police station let slip – strictly off the record – that the deceased's note was definitely in her own handwriting, and an overturned dining room chair lay on the hall floor near where her body was suspended.

Remarks by Tanice's family at the funeral had supported Michael Steggles' suggestion that the poor woman had somehow been "driven to it". There was no firm evidence to support the accusation, however, and it eventually faded from public consciousness.

A second rumour, that Mrs Lawrence was naked when she hanged herself, originated with Milena Jankowski from No 56. As Milena picked up a bottle of vodka from the shop every morning, her claim to have seen Tanice's body through the front door when the police entered the house was met with polite but disbelieving nods.

Slowly, as Christmas passed and the short grey days of winter lengthened imperceptibly towards spring, life on Shakespeare Avenue fell back into its accustomed channels. When Coleville Lawrence finally ventured out, five-and-a-half weeks after his wife's death, those who knew him offered muted and often embarrassed condolences. The first time he returned to the shop, Mrs Malhotra, in a gesture of neighbourly commiseration, even held his hand a little longer than was necessary as she handed him his change. He responded with a strange stare. Mrs M said it was the sort of look a fox gave when caught going through a rubbish bin. She explained it as shyness. Later, when chatting with Alice O'Connor, she said what Mr Lawrence now needed was a hobby, "something to take him out of himself".

Please, Tanice. Before you go. Just once.

I really don't want to, Cole.

Even when you know how much I love you? Darling Tanice! Please!

Must I?

For my sake, please!

If I have to. But promise it's the last time?

Promise.

The first sign that Coleville Lawrence had unwittingly heeded Mrs Mulhotra's advice was the arrival of a "signed for" parcel while he was at work. Alice scribbled her name on the electronic pad and took the heavy, rectangular package round that evening. She hoped it was something nice, she said as she handed it over. He replied that it was "just a camera" – a remark that prompted Alice's partner to suggest that Lawrence obviously wanted it to take "porno pix". Alice told him to give the man a chance.

Further parcels followed: from Amazon came *Teach Yourself Photography* and, a month later, a specialist supplier in Croydon sent two very expensive camera lenses. Michael Steggles' guess at Coleville's subject matter was way off target: every Saturday morning, whatever the weather, he emerged from his front door wearing a black anorak and carrying a large camera bag. From the bus stop in Fairfax Road he took the 64A out to Athelstan Ridge, an area of Outstanding Natural Beauty that began a couple of miles from the outskirts of the town.

It was not the Ridge's spectacular views that interested Coleville, nor its rocky summits. What he photographed as he tramped the muddy paths for hours on end were its trees. He was obsessed with them. Ancient oaks and beeches were his favourites, especially when he found one growing alone on a hillside. These proudly towering structures were to him symbols of power and independence; their thick trunks were firm, muscular bodies, their branches strong arms capable of bearing any weight.

At the end of May, Coleville joined the local photography club. He listened rather than spoke at meetings, and learned a lot about light and shade, colour, f-stops, shutter speeds and pixels. In June, he began showing his tree pictures to fellow members. The photographs were, it was universally agreed, remarkably good. He really ought to enter one or two in the summer exhibition they held in the town hall. Coleville thanked them and said he would.

You know how much this means to me, Tanice.

Be careful, Cole! Not too tight, please!

I'll always remember this, dearest Tanice.

Coleville Lawrence's "Strong Arms", an image of a solitary oak tree on Athelstan Ridge, was awarded second prize in the Teasbury Amateur Photography Club's annual exhibition. The Mayor, who opened the show with a few words written by his secretary about the importance of the arts in the modern world, was particularly taken by the picture. The Council was planning a "Green Week" for early September, and he wondered whether, to mark the occasion, Coleville might put on a small show of his tree photographs in the foyer of the Council offices? He would be paid a fee, of course, plus any reasonable expenses.

After a slight hesitation, Coleville accepted the invitation, and news of his forthcoming one-man exhibition made a small announcement in the local paper. Mrs Malhotra spotted it immediately. The effect on Coleville's reputation was swift and dramatic: within a few days, he went from being, in Charlie Slade's words, "That odd little bloke whose wife topped herself" to "the Cecil bleeding Beaton of Shakespeare Ave". Though most residents associated the name "Beaton" with cookery rather than photography, they took a strange pride in having a very minor local celebrity as a neighbour.

Only Michael Steggles refused to be impressed. He said that just because Lawrence took good pictures of trees, it didn't make him any less weird. In fact, he continued, taking photographs of trees was pretty weird in itself.

Alice told him to stop being so hard on the man.
Ow! That hurts!

I thought you liked it, Tanice?

No. It's not nice! Please hurry up.

At the Camera Club, Coleville had learned the importance of presentation. With the Council's fee he bought a top-of-the-range professional photo printer, a stock of the best photo paper, and acid-free mounting boards. He took a fortnight's holiday in August and used it to traipse over Athelstan Ridge taking hundreds of new pictures. He lay on the ground to find original angles and got up before dawn or waited until sunset to capture the changing light. Every evening, he downloaded the day's work onto his computer and went through the images to select the best.

By the end of his holiday, Coleville's "Top Trees" file contained twenty-four of his finest photographs. The next step was to print and mount them ready for public display.

No, Cole, no!

'But you love it, Tanice darling, don't you?'

I … can't … breathe …

The first photograph Coleville printed was of a young oak. Bent almost double by successive winter gales, it stood gaunt and defiant against a stormy sky. When the picture came out of the printer, Coleville examined it carefully, first with the naked eye then with a magnifying glass. Damn! There was a slight flaw, a minute dark spot beneath the lowest branch.

Coleville returned to the image on his computer screen and looked at it under maximum magnification, hoping that the fault was in one of the printer's ink cartridges or nozzles. But no. To his intense frustration, he found a cluster of rogue pixels on the original photograph. He checked a second picture and found the same thing. Strangely, the blemish was in the same position as in the photograph of the young oak – directly beneath the lowest branch.

Coleville swore and examined a third photograph. Whereas in the previous two the lowest branch had been on the left, this time it was on the right – and so was the blemish beneath it. It was as if the pixel cluster had deliberately moved to position itself under the branch.

There was obviously a loose speck of dust on the camera's mirror, Coleville reasoned, and it was pure chance that, at the moment he pressed the shutter, it happened to be where it was. Nevertheless, it was odd. All twenty-four photographs, whether of spreading beeches, ancient elms or blasted oaks, had precisely the same mark beneath their lowest branch. It was particularly frustrating because, with his exhibition only days away, Coleville couldn't possibly return to Athelstan Ridge and take a fresh set of pictures.

He looked at the photographs once more. The spots were disappointing, but they were so tiny that only an expert would be aware of them. Sharp-eyed members of the Camera Club might say something, as much out of jealousy as anything else, but no member of the public passing through the Council foyer would ever notice. Telling himself he was too much of a perfectionist for his own good, Coleville proceeded to mount his twenty-four pictures on the special white board.

God, I – love – you – so – much!

… stop … breathe …

When all the photographs were in place, Coleville realised there was something missing.

They were unnamed. He opened an online *Encyclopedia of Trees and Woods* and decided that, rather than opting for traditional Hearts-of-Oakstyle captions, he'd choose a single word starting with each letter of the alphabet, from A to X. Some, like "Ash", were easy because the tree was well-known. Others, like "Dule" (a tree that traditionally provided the wood for gallows) were trickier.

The Mayor planned to open the exhibition at 10 a.m. on the first Saturday in September. On returning from work the previous evening, Coleville wrapped his pictures in protective cardboard, carefully loaded them into a taxi, and went off with them to the Council offices. The caretaker was there to let him in, and stood chatting as he hung his photographs in alphabetical order on the specially provided stands. He then borrowed the caretaker's stepladder to redirect the ceiling spotlights so they shone directly on his pictures.

Finally, he stood back to admire his work. Yes, it certainly was a lovely display. Professional looking, too – apart from those blasted pixel clusters. He cursed them under his breath one last time before bidding the caretaker good night and returning home in a taxi.

Mr Lawrence, forensics say your wife had sexual intercourse shortly before her death. Could you tell us what you know about this?

Sexual intercourse? Yes, my wife was a very passionate woman. She often demanded that we made love before I left for work.

And that's what happened on the morning of her death?

After breakfast, yes. She was still in her nightdress.

I said I had to leave – but she insisted.

Against your wishes?

Yes. You see, I found it difficult. I think she found me disappointing …

Mrs Malhotra got her husband to look after the shop so she could catch the bus to the Council offices in time to be present when the Mayor opened Mr Lawrence's exhibition. She was looking forward to seeing his photographs, too. She didn't see many trees nowadays, she told Charlie Slade, being so busy in the shop. But she still found them pretty.

They were useful, too, Charlie replied. Shade, walking sticks, tables, wooden legs ... Mrs Malhotra told him not to be so cheeky.

She was at the far end of the foyer, near the door to the reception area, when Coleville Lawrence entered. At first, she hardly recognised him. He had restyled himself as an artist, swapping his grey suit and tie for navy blue chinos and a pink, open-necked shirt beneath a denim jacket. He'd allowed his thinning grey hair to grow long.

Mrs Malhotra watched, fascinated, as he shook hands with the Mayor and his deputy before turning towards the photographs on the stand beside him. What happened next, she said, would stay with her for the rest of her life.

Coleville Lawrence stood, hands dangling at his sides, staring at the photograph directly in front of him. It was "Dule", the fourth picture in the sequence. After looking at it for a full minute, his fingers started to twitch, and he moved on to the next photograph, "Elm". Then it was "Firelighter", followed by "Gallows" …

At this point, he spun round to face the small crowd gathered around the Mayor. Mrs Malhotra said his voice was no more than a hoarse whisper as he asked whether this was some sort of joke.

The room fell silent.

Now shaking quite violently, he repeated his question: was this some sort of sick joke?

The Mayor, clearly affronted by the unwarranted accusation, asked him what on earth he was talking about. He'd taken the photographs, hadn't he, and hung them himself the previous evening? Since then, no one had gone near them.

At this point, Mrs Malhotra reported, Coleville Lawrence "lost it". In a torrent of semi-coherent abuse aimed partly at people in the room and partly at what he called "a conspiracy of evil pixels", he demanded to know who was responsible for adding an image of his naked wife hanging by the neck from the lowest branch of every tree; not suspended by a dressing gown cord, either, but by a pair of hands with fingers like tinned asparagus.

The Hologram

Lord Ringsholt's divorce cost a great deal more than he had anticipated. Having paid the settlement and expenses, a painful meeting with his accountant revealed a seven-figure hole in his estate for which there was no obvious solution. Selling the early Constable and two Romneys would help, but to find the full sum he'd have to part with at least half of his stock market portfolio or reduce his farmland to a mere 50-acre rump around Ringsholt Hall. Both options would leave him, in his own words, "with almost nothing to live on".

He needed a plan.

The crisis meeting was attended by a senior partner from his accountancy firm, his stockbroker, his estate manager, and the new Lady Ringsholt. As well as being twenty-seven years younger and a great deal more attractive than the others in the room, Lady Julia's degree in arts management made her better qualified to come up with a solution to her husband's difficulties.

What was his greatest single asset? The Hall, of

course. *Was he maximising its potential?* There had been a steady trickle of visitors since it opened to the public in 1956 – as many as 30 or 40 on a good day – and they had recently converted the stables into a tearoom … *In other words,* she interrupted, *no.*

The answer, Lady Julia insisted, was to turn Ringsholt Hall into an "attraction". The peer winced at the word but bowed to his wife's superior knowledge in such matters. It would take a bit of capital, of course, but she was sure the bank would stump up if shown a sound business plan. She was right. Funding was forthcoming for a miniature railway, a small zoo, a country crafts centre, and a restaurant suite available for outside functions. The newly appointed publicity manager, twenty-five-year-old Theresa Accrington-Smith, arranged widespread media coverage, and visitor numbers soared.

Lady Julia also revamped what she called the *visitor experience* within the Hall itself. Audio guides were installed, the Victorian kitchen refurbished, the displays reorganised and recaptioned to emphasise the scandalous and the sensational. As a pièce de résistance she created a new "Chamber of Horror", dedicated to Sir Richard Featherstone, a 17th-century ancestor of the present baronet who had been executed by one of Cromwell's Major-Generals for a string of gruesome rapes and murders.

The Chamber's centrepiece was a state-of-the-art hologram depicting the murderer. It was designed and installed by Digital Veracity (DV), a London-based company that had already set up similar historical figures in the Tower of London and Dover Castle. DV's chief engineer, the brilliant young Harry Kermode, worked directly from the portrait in the Great Hall. Further details were added by Lady Julia, who wrote the faux 17th-century script for the device's unique voice response system.

"What fun it would be if the thing could talk," she had suggested to Harry one day when they were working on the design. "Perhaps you could get Sir Richard to say who he was and a bit about what he'd done. Maybe even answer a few questions."

Harry rose to the challenge and fitted the display with an Alexa-style voice-recognition chip, microphones and speakers. Although a bit clunky at first, he explained that over time it would become more realistic. During testing, the voices of Lord Ringsholt, Theresa and an estate gardener were fed into the machine and stored.

Sir Richard's electronic accent came out as a curious blend of aristocratic drawl and rural Shropshire, while a sprinkling of thees and thous lent his vocabulary a sort of Biblical authenticity. The combination proved remarkably effective, especially when the machine's laser eyes fixed upon a young woman. Then, as Sir Richard's lips parted in a sensuous smile, he would declare unctuously, "'Pon my word, thou art the fairest damsel that ever I had the pleasure to set mine eyes upon. Woulds't thou care to call upon me at the Hall?"

A few visitors, mainly teenage girls, found this sort of approach a little too realistic. They described the lifelike behaviour of the laser-generated figure as "weirdly attractive" yet at the same time "creepy" and "threatening". When Theresa told Lady Julia that she understood what they meant, she met with a light-hearted, "Oh grow up, Theresa! That's the whole point, isn't it?" She pointed out that the great majority of visitors were delighted with the Chamber, invariably awarding it five stars on the visitor satisfaction survey on Ringsholt Hall's revamped website.

Before encountering it, visitors walked by large, illustrated panels setting out Sir Richard's story under the eye-catching heading, "The Ripper of Ringsholt Hall". Lady Julia, with the reluctant assistance of her publicity manager, Theresa, assembled the text by splicing together extracts from the County Court records and snippets of local legend.

The story told by the panels was this. Sir Richard, the younger brother of the 3rd baronet, had assumed charge of the Hall when his elder brother went into exile with the future King Charles II. As the portrait in the Great Hall bore witness, the twenty-two-year-old aristocrat was extremely good looking. He was also evil. His deviancy was hard to explain, for the Featherstones were not a brutal family and his father had married his mother on account of her exceptionally sweet nature. Talk of an early love affair that had gone wrong was hardly sufficient to explain what followed.

For six successive months, at the time of the full moon, a maiden from within the County of

Shropshire disappeared. They were all pretty, aged about eighteen, and known to be virgins. At the end of the seventh month, a couple who lived in the village nearest to the Hall were woken in the middle of the night by terrified screaming and hammering on their door. They hurried downstairs to find their eldest daughter, whom they had believed to be safe in bed, standing naked before them. She had been subjected to a vicious and perverted assault that would leave her permanently disabled in body and mind.

The following afternoon, calmed by sleep and half a bottle of French brandy, the poor girl was able to put together a somewhat garbled account of what had happened. Over the previous few days, Sir Richard had part-bullied, part-seduced her into going to meet him at the Hall. Only when she got inside did she realise his intentions were anything but romantic. She was gagged, raped and beaten. Worse was to follow, but somehow she managed to flee through a window when her torturer stooped to sharpen his knife.

Major-General James Berry was a stern but fair man of a puritanical disposition. When the wretched girl's story was brought to his attention, he immediately ordered Sir Richard Featherstone to be detained and Ringsholt Hall thoroughly searched. The decayed and mutilated corpses of the missing girls were found buried beneath the floor of the wine cellar. When faced with such overwhelming evidence of his guilt, Sir Richard is reported to have "let out a laugh of such evil as though the Devil himself were within his bowels", and freely admitted his guilt.

Still laughing, he was hanged a week later.

Given the popularity of similarly macabre displays in other attractions around the country, it should come as no surprise that Ringsholt Hall's Chamber of Horror was a tremendous success. Lady Julia estimated that a thousand people a day passed through it in the first week. In the second, the number doubled and a booking system had to be introduced.

Then, in the middle of the third week, came the terrible tragedy, and the attraction was closed.

Early on the Wednesday morning, the naked body of Theresa Accrington-Smith was discovered in a pool of blood on the Chamber floor. Forensic examination confirmed she had been the victim of a particularly brutal rape and murder. As well as being assaulted sexually, she had been subjected to a series of excruciating tortures, including being repeatedly bitten on her chest and legs. She finally died, perhaps an hour after the first assault, when her attacker cut her throat.

The police categorised the crime as an unpleasant example of a copycat killing, the perpetrator having followed the example set out in the panels on the Chamber's walls. Their suspicions may well have been correct. However, as DNA and dental tests failed to come up with anything and no one was ever apprehended, doubts remained. In support of these, let me draw your attention to two facts never put before the police or coroner, facts that suggest a different and altogether more sinister interpretation of what happened that dark night in Ringsholt Hall's fatal attraction.

The first piece of information not available to the coroner was that Harry Kermode and Theresa Accrington-Smith had history. The couple had met in their final year of university and fallen madly in love. Their romance followed the usual course for people of their age, with one important exception: Theresa, a fervent Roman Catholic, had vowed not to sleep with anyone before she was engaged to be married. Harry respected her wish and the unconsummated affair continued smoothly through to their final exams in May.

A week later, the couple went for a celebratory weekend at the Golden Lamb, a fashionable and very expensive country hotel near Bath. As they booked a double room, they both knew what would happen. Harry, whose university education had proved a constant financial strain on himself and his parents, took out a loan to buy a fiendishly expensive diamond engagement ring. He had already worked out that the hotel bill would max out his credit card. But it was worth it, he told himself – you only get engaged once.

The dinner and the wine were delicious. After the dishes had been cleared away and they were gazing into each other's eyes, thinking of what lay ahead, Harry presented Theresa with the ring and asked her to marry him. *Yes*, she said. *Yes, yes, yes!* They were engaged.

They retired to their room shortly afterwards. When Harry went into the bathroom to clean his teeth, Theresa, as she had done every day of her life, knelt by the side of the bed to say her prayers.

What passed between herself and the Blessed Virgin we will never know, but the upshot was that Harry returned to find her preparing a makeshift bed for herself on the floor. She was very sorry, she explained, but she had changed her mind. It would not be right to have sex with someone before she was married.

A massive row ensued. He called her a frigid cow, to which she responded that he was an insensitive chauvinist bastard. When she returned her engagement ring, he opened the window and hurled it out into the night, declaring that he had no interest in tainted goods. With that, he packed his bag, stomped downstairs, and checked out. As they had come in her car, he endured the added ignominy of having to wait for a taxi to take him to the station where he slept on the platform until the first train the following morning.

The couple had no further contact until, five years later, the DV van drew up outside Ringsholt Hall and Harry stepped out to install the new hologram. They recognised each other immediately, though neither gave any sign, then or later, that they knew one another.

The artificial "brain" Harry installed in his

creation in the Chamber of Horror was more sophisticated than any he had used previously. Was it out of malice that he used Theresa's profile when programming it? And why, after he had dismantled it, did he leave DV, swearing never to work with holograms or artificial intelligence ever again?

Theresa was concerned by the display from the moment it was first switched on. She found it simultaneously abhorrent yet wickedly alluring, and could have sworn its eyes followed her as she walked around the room. On one occasion, Lady Julia found her employee talking to it and later mentioned Theresa's strange obsession to the police. They assumed it was why she was in the Chamber on the night the copycat killer struck.

'The attacker must have been turned on by the whole set-up,' mused the detective in charge of the case. 'So he goes back one night to get his weird kicks and finds Ms Accrington-Smith there. The rest we know, except our maniac adds a bit of his own special nastiness by biting her.'

Which brings us to the second piece of information not available to the coroner. When Theresa was researching the story of Sir Richard in the County library, she came across a legend telling how he bit his victims repeatedly on the chest and legs before cutting their throats. Believing it was too upsetting a detail for inclusion on the Chamber panels, she kept the discovery to herself.

Keeping in Touch

Whenever I ask my students to write about someone they admire, a good twenty-five percent choose a grandparent. That would not be my choice. My father's parents were killed when their Morris Traveller ran into a tree beside the A303 before I was born, leaving my mother's parents, Grandpa Gilbert and Grandma Sally, my only link with the generation of rationing and "illegitimate" children. It was not a link I enjoyed.

This was, I suppose, partly my fault. As a child I kept my feelings to myself, eager to please even if it meant sheltering behind a screen of white lies about Grandpa's leering, bloodshot eyes, Grandma's disgusting breath, and their seemingly pathological inability to keep their hands off each other. When, around the age of seven or eight, I asked why my grandparents were not like other people's, my mother told me not to ask silly questions. Grandpa and Grandma were quite normal, she said airily, just "special" people with a very "touching" love for each other. The word was certainly appropriate, though not as she meant it.

One particular stomach-churning episode remains with me. It was in the summer holidays at the end of my first year at secondary school. As I had never been brave enough to express the strength of my revulsion at the company of Grandpa and Grandma, my parents asked them to look after me for a couple of weeks while they went on holiday to some exotic location – I forget where – they said was not suitable for a boy of my age.

Before getting back into the car with my mother and driving off to Heathrow, my father, in the nearest he ever came to admitting that he shared my dislike of his parents-in-law, patted me on the arm and muttered something about it taking all sorts and treating it as part of my education. An education it certainly was. I was a relatively naïve twelve-year-old, and what I saw and, particularly, what I heard, during the ensuing two weeks seared itself into my mind with the permanent intensity of a branding. I have never married – the stroking, licking, whispered obscenities, and up-skirt, through-fly caressing of a pair of sixty-five-year-olds so sickened me that to this day I have never enjoyed intimate relations with a fellow human being. Nor was it just the physical behaviour that distressed me. There was something sinister, almost demonic, about their mutual infatuation. Like creatures from Dante's hell, they appeared doomed to re-enact for ever the sins of their damnation. The scene is my recurring nightmare: me, sitting in a greasy armchair before the flickering television, torn between studied disinterest and adolescent prurience, while only feet away my desiccated grandparents re-enacted scenes from Hieronymus Bosch. While he was her "Dirty Bertie", she was his "Naughty Little Sis" – terms of endearment that, even as I write, make me shudder.

The fortnight passed, my parents returned, and I replied with a polite "yes" when asked if I had had a good time. How could I have said anything else? Some of my school friends admitted openly to discussing everything at the supper table – Charlie Templeton even said they talked about sex – but not us. It was as if the extreme public license of my grandparents obliged the next generation to go the other way, drawing a curtain of embarrassed respectability across intimate discussion with their only child. Had I had brothers and sisters, it might have been different.

In due course, I took a degree and qualified as an English teacher. During that time, I saw little of my grandparents, but when my mother and father retired to Spain and I got a post in Novey Gladbourne Academy, only twenty miles from Sherford, where my ancient relatives lived, I felt obliged as a dutiful grandson to call in from time to time. I never stayed long.

Neither Grandpa nor Grandma ever had much time for housework. Now, approaching their dotage, they shuffled around their dark and foetid-smelling cottage, half-naked and never more than a few inches apart, like robotic moles whose batteries were about to give out. They maintained their obsessive fumblings, though they were less vigorous now – more like shoppers at a fruit stall checking the wares for ripeness. The cottage curtains were permanently closed over grimy windows, post piled like leaves on the floor behind the front door, pillars of dirty dishes rose unsteadily out of the greasy sink, and the putrid foulness of the toilet would have disgraced a Victorian slum. I brought food, cleaned as much as I could manage in about twenty minutes, and left with such washing as I could bring myself to pick up.

On the drive home, with the car windows wound down to diffuse the stench of the foul clothes on the back seat, I invariably pondered on the personalities of the aged couple I had just visited, and the nature of their obsessive relationship. At school, at college and in the staff room I had watched couples fall in love. I had seen – and, if I am honest, longed to be able to experience for myself – the lingering glances, secret caresses, and smiles of unalloyed happiness. In every case, what struck me most was the lovers' inescapable joy at their mutual enslavement. It was something even the most leaden-headed Year Seven pupil picked up as they wrestled with the antique expression of love's magical and transformative power in *Romeo and Juliet*. But in my grandparents' behaviour I saw little of that joy. If their relationship was magical, it was a dark, twisted sort of magic emanating not from within their hearts but from some outside force. What this was, I had no idea back them. In the light of what was to happen, however, I have suspicions that scare me.

How did such an introverted and unworldly

couple survive? As I have mentioned, I did what I could to keep their home more or less habitable. Over time, I found myself managing their pensions, too, making sure they had enough cash for their weekly potter down to the small supermarket-cum Post Office on the corner of their street. Mr Shah, the franchise holder, knew them well and stepped in when they forgot to pick up a regular item, or politely removed from their basket something he knew they did not need.

'It's alright, Mr Stephen,' he said when I called to thank him for these small acts of kindness. 'I understand. My mother said that in the village where she was born there was a couple just like your grandparents. They were called "the Children of Rati" – because they had sold their souls and bodies to Her.'

'I'm sorry, Mr Shah, but who's Rati?'

He chuckled. 'In the West you usually call her the goddess of love. I think that's being polite. "Lust" is a better word.'

I frowned. 'You believe that stuff, Mr Shah? I mean about people selling themselves to some sex goddess?'

'Not really, Mr Stephen. Most likely ignorant

superstition. Just village nonsense.'

I took his word for it. Nevertheless, out of curiosity I googled Rati when I got home. All the sites were pretty-near unanimous: a sensuous, lusty, uninhibited, beautiful Hindu goddess associated with sexual positions, bodily fluids and even incest. One image of her – a multicoloured buxom woman riding a horse made up of five other smiling women – I would come across later.

Well-meaning neighbours kept an eye and let me know when minor repairs, like unblocking a drainpipe or replacing a fallen roof tile, were needed. "Trimmers", a local gardening business, kept the lawn and flowerbeds from getting too overgrown, and – from time to time – social services popped in to make sure the couple were coping. On one of these visits, a young inspector, distressed by the squalor in which they lived, bravely suggested they move into a local care home. Her idea met with such a torrent of invective and tearful distress that she immediately backed down. She reported back to her line manager that for the time being, supported by their grandson and others in the community, Mr and Mrs Nixon were able to continue living independently.

A month later, the neighbours were woken in the middle of the night by a terrible howling emanating from my grandparents' house. When their knocks on the door brought neither response nor a diminution of the ghastly din, they called me. I threw on some clothes, picked up my spare key and hurried over to Sherford to see what was happening. Though the death of my eighty-five-year-old grandfather was hardly a surprise, the same could not be said of my grandmother's reaction to it. On the journey there, I had anticipated some sort of tragedy, and steeled myself for desperate weeping and wailing. But what I encountered at 3.30 am on that dreadful night was far beyond anything I could have imagined.

Picture a gaunt, eighty-four-year-old woman, her shrivelled skin a translucent yellowy-white, sitting in the dark on one end of a grubby sofa. Wearing only threadbare pyjama bottoms, on her lap she cradles the head of the corpse stretched out on the sofa beside her. Dried blood crusts around its nose and mouth. From time to time she reaches out a hand and strokes the emaciated body beneath its dirty string vest.

The scene itself – a grim parody of a pièta

– is grisly enough. The actions and noises of my grandmother make it truly terrible. With a mechanical regularity, she raises her face, partly hidden behind lank grey hair, lifts unseeing eyes, and lets out a long, animal-like howl.

Even now, I tremble at the memory of it.

The noise stopped only when a doctor arrived and gave her a sedative. We took her upstairs and put her to bed. The doctor, the neighbours and I cleaned my grandfather's body, made it respectable and laid it out respectfully on the sofa. It was taken away by an undertaker early the next morning.

I rang the school at 8 am to explain why I would not be in for the next day or two, and then called my parents. My mother answered the phone. I spared her the ghastly details, telling her only that her father had passed away peacefully in the night. For a moment or two she did not respond. When she did it was simply to observe "so that's the end of that" and ask me if I would be good enough to deal with the formalities as Sally – she had referred to her parents by their first names for as long as I could remember – would not be able to cope.

I agreed, of course, and said I'd let her know the

date of the funeral as soon as it had been arranged. What a relief it was in situations like this, she prattled, to have a nice sensible son to handle all the tedious business of certificates and so on. Her flattery was unconvincing; I suspected, correctly as it turned out, that it was a prelude to something less straightforward.

'You don't mind, do you Stephen?' she continued, sounding less breezily assured. 'I mean, you never know what you might find going through old papers and things.'

I told her not to worry. As a teacher, I was used to sorting out mountains of paperwork. After a few hurried words of thanks, she rang off. She and dad were expected round at their neighbours' for their weekly rubber of bridge.

Later that morning, I opened the large cardboard box in which my grandparents kept their papers. They were in good order, though I was surprised to find, on top of everything else, a framed, poor-quality reproduction of the goddess Rati on horseback – the same image I'd found during my Google search. I was even more surprised to see it'd been signed: "Our pledge, Sally and Gilbert Nixon, 4th July 1950." I am neither religious nor superstitious; nevertheless, recalling Mr Shah's remark about "Children of Rati" who sold their souls and bodies to the lascivious goddess, I was taken aback. My grandparents were stranger than I'd realised. In their youth they must have got involved in some sort of hippy-style sex cult, and then stuck with it. I gazed at the picture, trying to imagine my grandparents signing it all those years ago. Had they been in India? If so, why were they there?

After a few minutes' fruitless speculation, I set the picture aside and dug out Grandpa's birth certificate. It had been issued in 1934. Flicking through the fragile brown envelopes in search of my Grandma's certificate, which I was sure I'd need before long, my eye was caught by a neat bundle marked "Adoption Papers". The perished rubber band holding it together snapped as soon as I picked it up, and I scanned through the documents that slipped onto the table.

Shock at what they revealed rapidly gave way to anger at my mother for not telling me the truth: I had been devoting a great deal of time to the care of people who, contrary to what I had been led to believe, were not my grandparents. Mr Gilbert

Nixon and Mrs Winifred Nixon had adopted the three-year-old Jennifer Wilmore, my mother, in 1954. Why had I not been told? My sense of having been cheated was so overwhelming that I paid scant attention to the forename discrepancy. As I had always known Grandma as "Sally", I assumed that long ago she'd decided that was how she wished to be known, rather than the more old-fashioned Winifred.

I resisted the temptation to call my mother and harangue her for having deceived me about her parentage. After all, I told myself, it really was none of my business. In fact, after a few hours my rage was replaced by an altogether more positive emotion. Relief.

'Thank God!' I found myself muttering. 'Thank God!'

There was no possibility that I, nor any children I might one day father, would inherit their great-grandparents' unsavoury personalities. Their family's sickness – for I was sure that's what I was – would perish with them. Consoled by this, I didn't mention the adoption to my parents when they returned for the funeral. Even if I had wanted to, there was little opportunity. They arrived by an early morning flight to Stanstead and reached the crematorium at the same time as the coffin. At my mother's request, I escorted Grandma Sally (despite what I knew, I couldn't bring myself to think of her as simply "Mrs Nixon") during the brief and empty ceremony. My parents sat together at the back. They brought no flowers, showed no signs of grief, and left in their rented car – "so sorry, Stephen, but it'll cost us a fortune if we don't get it back by six" as soon as the formalities were over. Neither of them said a word to Grandma. Heavily sedated, she drifted through the event in a semi-coma, aware of neither the proceedings nor the presence of my parents.

There was no wake. After the funeral, I thanked the undertakers and the two neighbours who had taken the trouble to attend (Mr Shah apologised later for his absence, saying he's been unable to leave the shop), and ushered Grandma to the car through the throng waiting for the arrival of the next cortege. We spoke not a word. I glanced across at her once or twice as I drove her back to Sherford. She sat like a life-size doll, moving not a muscle of her own volition but swaying gently in her seatbelt as we went round corners. On arrival,

I all but carried her upstairs and put her to bed.

I managed everything. I don't say this with any sense of pride, but simply because it bears on the extraordinary events of the next few weeks. I collected the death certificate, arranged for a conventional inscription in the crematorium's Book of Remembrance, and, with Mr Shah's help, sorted out Grandma's widow's pension. A few days after the funeral, I collected Grandpa's ashes, grey-white dust inside a plastic bag, bought a tacky fake gold urn to store them in, and took them round to Grandma's.

She was no longer sedated and had made a full physical recovery from the shock of her partner's death. But her mind seemed so dislocated from reality that I was starting to wonder whether she had suffered some sort of instantaneous-onset dementia. When I knocked on her front door, I heard her shuffling rapidly towards it calling plaintively, 'Bertie? Is that you, Bertie? Ah, wicked Bertie to keep your Naughty Little Sis waiting all this time!'

Faces are often described as "falling" with disappointment. As she opened the door, dressed in a dirty nightgown, my grandma's face did not fall so much as petrify. It became a plaster-of-Paris mask, hard, white, immobile. Within it, her eyes stared with an unsettling mix of disappointment and fury.

The plaster cracked enough for her to speak. 'You? Where's Bertie? What have you done with him?'

My mind is of the careful, steady sort. While I like to think I have a certain wisdom, I'm the first to admit that swift assessment is not my forte. That explains – but does not excuse – my reply. Confronted by my grandma's ridiculous accusation, I held out the golden urn and said with what I hoped was reassuring bonhomie, 'Don't worry, Grandma. Here he is!'

At first, she did not respond. 'It's Grandpa's ashes,' I explained. 'I thought you might like –'

Before I could finish the sentence, she seized the urn with surprising strength and clutched it to her chest. 'Bertie!' she sighed. 'Darling Bertie!' She rubbed the urn against her shrunken chest. 'Lovely Dirty Bertie!'

My old disgust flooded back, and I turned away. When her obscene cackles had subsided to a hoarse whisper, I asked her where the urn should be kept. Another mistake. It took me ten minutes and a string of white lies to persuade her that the mantlepiece – where she could stare at Bertie all day long – was a more fitting resting place than her bed. I left her sitting on the sofa, her eyes fixed on the plastic urn with the intensity of a nun before a statue of her crucified Lord.

I visited the following day and twice more that week. On each occasion, I found my grandmother alert and coping remarkably well. There was a sparkle in her eye I had not seen before, and I dismissed as foolish my previous dementia worries. A depression on the sofa told me she spent many hours contemplating the urn, but I was relieved to see she had also been leafing through the pile of magazines I'd brought her. One lay open at an article about the usefulness of mobile phones for the elderly. She'd clearly read it and taken in what it said, for when I asked her if there was anything she needed, she replied firmly, 'Yes, one of those mobile phone things. So I can get in touch with… you and everyone else.'

'You mean Mr Shah?'

'Yes, Mr Shah.' She paused with her head slightly to one side, reminding me of a child when forced to think up a quick excuse. 'He's such a kind man. I could phone him and ask him to bring my groceries.'

'Maybe, yes. The main thing is, a phone would be useful in an emergency. If you had a fall for example. You could call me – or anyone – wherever you were.'

She liked this idea. 'Speak to anyone, Stephen, wherever I was?'

'Yes, Grandma.'

'Ah! Bring me a mobile phone, there's a good boy.'

I did as she asked. Although the cheapest I could find, it fulfilled her basic requirements. I explained how it worked, about voice calls, texts and the need to keep it charged, and added my number and Mr Shah's to the memory. I thought about adding my mother's but decided against it. Grandma Sally was not her birthmother, and her "that's the end of that" remark had sounded very final. No, my mother would not want a call in the small hours telling her that Mrs Nixon was feeling unwell.

As soon as I got home, I rang Grandma to check she understood how her phone worked. She responded with surprising speed. A text evoked a similarly swift response. I didn't call again that week; neither did she.

The reason became clear when I dropped in at the weekend. She had lost her new phone. This annoyed me. A teacher does not have money to throw around and I couldn't believe an old woman who never left the house could possibly lose a phone. When calling the number brought no response, I questioned her again. My words were harsher than I intended. Weeping like a figure in a cartoon movie, she knelt before me, grabbed my hand between both of hers, and pleaded, 'Please get me another one, dearest Stephen. I am so sorry. Your old Grandma is so sorry. Please! Please! Please –'

I pulled my hand away in disgust. 'Alright Grandma. One more. But only if you promise to look after it, ok?'

Remaining on her knees, she looked up at me with bright, glistening eyes. 'Yes, dearest Stephen. I will guard it with my life. Thank you! You don't know…' A far-away look came across her face as she left the sentence unfinished.

I brought a second phone, identical to the first,

fitted a new SIM card and took it round to Sherford on Wednesday evening. Once more, I called and texted to make sure she knew how to work it, then left her for ten days. She could call me if she wanted anything, and I needed a break from my duties as an unofficial social worker. The following week was half term, and I'd decided to clear my head by taking a walking holiday, alone, in the Lake District. The broad vistas and fresh mountain air did me good and I did not get home until late on Sunday.

After school the next day, I drove over to see how Grandma was getting on. I knew instinctively what to expect as soon as my knock on the door brought no response. She lay sprawled at the foot of the stairs, her head twisted backwards at an impossible angle. The deep gash on her forehead, ringed with dried blood, exposed the ivory bone of her skull. The post-mortem examination would give the cause of death as a broken neck and severe blow to the head concomitant with falling headlong downstairs two days previously. Each injury was severe enough by itself to have caused her death.

I dialled 999 and waited for the emergency

services to arrive. Gazing at the distorted wreck of a human being, I pondered – as one tends to do in such situations – the futility of life and the bleak negativity of death. All that effort, the tears and smiles, the pointless love … At which point, I noticed her mobile phone lying on the floor a few feet from the body. It must have been in her hand as she fell. I wondered if she had been trying to call me. Curiosity got the better of circumspection (surely no one could charge me with murder!), and I picked up the phone. It still worked and had 57% battery left. *Well done Grandma!* I smiled. At least you remembered to keep it charged.

As I examined the screen more carefully, my mood changed. No, not well done! It was her old phone, the one she said she had lost. *You lying old…* It had been used every day since I gave it to her.

Someone had called her each morning at 11.45 precisely. The same caller every time. The calls lasted about ten minutes. Roughly thirty seconds after they ended, the caller texted her. The message was always the same, "Hurry! I'm waiting!"

I looked closely at the caller's number. It seemed familiar. I took out my own phone and checked. Good God! It was the number of her new phone, the second one I'd bought her. She'd wanted another phone so she could call and send messages to herself!

I was trying to work out what all this meant when the police and ambulance arrived, and I was caught up in answering the necessary questions, providing details, and so forth. Some forty-five minutes later, the ambulance departed with the body; the police – convinced that nothing untoward had occurred – left me to lock up the house and drive home.

Now I understood the business with the two phones, I realized Grandma had never been anything but alert and compos mentis – wickedly so. She had lied about losing the phone so she could acquire a second one to continue a fictional version of her nauseating relationship with my grandpa. I imagined her sitting there with a phone in each hand, calling herself with one phone then responding with the other. Did she used different voices, I wondered, one for herself and one for Grandpa? When she had finished the conversation, she sent herself a text.

No, her illness was not dementia. Together. with her late husband, in her youth she had joined some kinky, pseudo-oriental cult that had locked them both into an insane and twisted obsession. I had witnessed it all those years ago and it had continued throughout their lives to the point where she had not allowed death itself to cut the filthy cord that tied her to her darling Dirty Bertie. Had she fallen downstairs or jumped? The daily message she sent to herself – "Hurry! I'm waiting!" – persuaded me it had been suicide. But I couldn't suggest this to the authorities. What would be the point? No one would believe me.

I returned to Sherfield after school the following day. The second phone was where I expected, inside the golden urn containing Grandpa's ashes. I took it out and checked the call list to confirm my theory. Yes, Grandma had used it to call her other phone at 11.45 each morning. And shortly after she'd ended the make-believe duologue, she'd used it to send the daily "Hurry!" message. I sighed, put the phone back in the urn and replaced the lid. As soon as the funeral was over, I resolved to make a bonfire of my grandparents' useless possessions. The hideous urn would take pride of place on the top, a guy, a totem of their repellent obsession.

As for the other phone, I'd get the undertaker to put it in Grandma's coffin so it would burn up alongside her. Only fire, I decided, could expunge the memory of my grandparents' behaviour. Ashes to ashes.

I think, as I wrote those last sentences, I was allowing myself to be influenced by hindsight. I had found their relationship repellent, but what I found next, after replacing the phone in the urn and turning to the box of family papers, made me retch with disgust.

Had I not been distracted by the discovery of my mother's adoption papers, I would have found the pair of brown packets at the bottom of the box during my previous inspection. Though the two envelopes were identical, the documents they contained were starkly different. Sickeningly, though, they complemented each other – the last two pieces of a surreal jigsaw. The first, dated 12 August 1935, was the birth certificate of Miss Sally Nixon. The other was a death certificate. It was dated 18 November 1975 and the name of the deceased was Mrs Winifred Nixon, wife of Mr Gilbert Nixon. The results of my Google search flashed before my mind: the goddess Rati was associated with sexual positions, bodily fluids and even incest…

My parents knew, of course. When I challenged them during our brief five minutes together before Grandma's funeral, my mother attempted to fob me off with a flurry of defensive platitudes. Whether this was insensitivity or a cloak for her guilt, I've no idea.

'What a relief, eh!' she began, fixing her gaze at the Garden of Remembrance over my left shoulder. 'It is easier all round now you know. Did take you a bit of time to cotton on, though, didn't it? I got it pretty much straight away. Reg says I've got a nose for these things. It still freaked me out, I can tell you. Talk about kinky! I mean, not just the sex bit. They were obsessed, weren't they? Like they couldn't help it.'

I tried to stop her. 'You knew, Mum, and yet you sent me –'

'Let me finish, Stephen. I've got my side to the story, haven't I? Reg got me out. I was sixteen and messed up; he was twenty-four and had a Sunbeam Alpine. That was it – end of.' She made an infantile attempt at a giggle. 'Or perhaps I should say beginning of, eh Reg?'

I couldn't take any more. 'Listen, Mum! Do you know what you're saying? You *knew*! You *knew* when you let me, your son, a shy and impressionable twelve-year-old, stay in a household stinking of superstitious sex and obsessive incest?'

'Don't be so hoity-toity, Stephen. You needed a bit of toughening up.'

I turned away to see the hearse carrying Grandma's coffin coming down the drive towards the crematorium. Since that moment, I have never spoken to my mother or father. And I never will.

I walked into the chapel with Mr Shah. Apart from the chaplain and my parents skulking at the back, we were the only congregation. We stood and watched in silence – I had requested no music – as the undertakers brought in Grandma's coffin with studied solemnity. I stared at the polished wooden box and tried to imagine the emaciated figure inside with a mobile phone clasped in its claw-like fingers – that was my specific instruction to the undertaker: in her hand, not just somewhere in the box. It was a macabre idea, but it seemed somehow appropriate. Looking back, I shudder to think how appropriate it was.

The chaplain finished her short and

inappropriate eulogy and pressed the button for the curtains to close and the coffin to roll into the furnace. The silence was broken only by the quiet whirr of the electric motor.

'Thank God that's over!' I muttered, looking sideways at Mr Shah.

He smiled. 'I hope so, Mr Stephen.'

'Eh?'

The curtains were halfway across, shutting inexorably over my past.

'My mother said Children of Rati never die.'

The edges of the curtain were almost touching now.

'Just village non –'

His whisper was interrupted by a faint ringing. As my own phone was switched off, I glanced at Mr Shah.

'Yours?' I mouthed.

He shook his head and nodded towards the coffin.

Beads of sweat broke out on my forehead. With a trembling hand, I pushed back my shirt cuff and looked at my watch.

11.45 am.

Heat Pump

My dear Bishop

IN STRICTEST CONFIDENCE

I understand from your secretary that you would like to hear from anyone with information regarding the tragic (and mysterious) disaster that struck Lower Tangthorpe two days ago. I am still unclear in my mind exactly what happened. Writing this email, therefore, will oblige me to sort out my own thoughts in order to pass them on to yourself. This will inevitably involve a bit of "thinking on the hoof", so please forgive me if I am not wholly consistent or coherent.

Let me state my position at the outset. Almost alone among the residents of the parish, I mistrusted Rev Mary Chumleigh from the moment she arrived. She was too worldly, too frank, too challenging to be a good priest. If pressed, I would even go further: I was never convinced of her faith in Almighty God. In truth, there were occasions when I feared that she was taking Our Lord's injunction to "love your enemy" rather too literally.

This is, I fully understand, a very serious

accusation. Nevertheless, I hope what I am about to say will demonstrate its plausibility.

You are well aware, Bishop, of the parlous state of the parishes of Lower Tangthorpe, Pangbury and Kelm at the beginning of this year. Following the death of Rev Simon Jacobson, we had had no rector of our own for eighteen long months. A number of well-meaning stand-ins and locums had done their best to maintain the pattern of divine service, but most were elderly and, in several cases, infirm. You may recall how, in December, the 78-year-old Rev Jeremiah Woolfson suffered a minor stroke while delivering a sermon during evensong at Pangbury.

In all three parishes, the congregations had dwindled to a mere handful of pensioners. Even at the normally popular "midnight masses" on Christmas Eve the pews were only half full. In the words of that great Anglican poet T.S. Elliot, our world was ending not with a bang but a whimper.

The situation in Lower Tangthorpe was worst of all. On one distressing Sunday in early January, the congregation assembled for Matins numbered just four: myself, Mrs Wynmore-Russell, and the two elderly ladies who rented the cottage on our farm.

The priest from another parish who had promised to officiate failed to turn up, and the service was abandoned.

I distinctly remember looking around as I left the church. St Michael and All Angels, which had served the faithful since the twelfth century, was almost a ruin. Patches of black mould disfigured the inside walls, and when it rained three orange plastic buckets had to be brought out from the vestry to catch the leaks. The cold was dreadful. The old, oil-fired boiler had given up the ghost a year before. Thereafter, the only heating – woefully inadequate – was provided by three electric radiators that we could afford to switch on barely half an hour before a service began.

Mice had attacked the rack of information leaflets and postcards near the door, so it had to be removed. Damp curled the pages of the hymn and prayer books. Even if we had an organist, the instrument was so out of tune that it could not be played. In January, we were obliged to cancel the only baptism for over a year because the water in the font had frozen solid. Our spirits, Bishop, were very low indeed.

At that point, around noon on 14 February, Rev

Mary Chumleigh arrived – and the transformation began. It started even before she had spoken a word to any member of her parish. As the removal men were unloading their lorry outside the rectory, Penny Librini happened to walk past on her way to the village shop. A young woman in a short denim skirt was laughing and telling the men that the double bed should go under the window in the room on the left at the top of the stairs. From there, she explained, she would be able to "check out talent" on the road outside from beneath her duvet. Mrs Librini was understandably fascinated. When she reached the shop, she told Mrs Kermode, who was behind the till at the time, that the new rector's daughter looked as if she was "a bit of a tearaway".

Five minutes later, the young woman in the short denim skirt entered the shop. She shook Mrs Kermode warmly by the hand, and introduced herself as Mary Chumleigh, "your new rector". Two days later, the Sunday service attracted a congregation of fifteen, not all of whom were over the age of fifty. When word got around that the title of her sermon, to be reprinted in the newly resurrected parish magazine, was "Sin, ancient and modern", the congregation on the following Sunday had risen to an astonishing forty-three. It was the highest number for twenty years.

I was, of course, pleased by these figures. I was equally pleased when they produced material benefit: the collection bags, which I passed round during the third hymn, garnered almost fifty pounds. Ms Chumleigh said it would have been a great deal more if we had replaced the "silly little bags" with contactless card payments. When she introduced this change two months later, the average donation rose from 75p to £4.50. As by then the congregation size was close to 100, St Michael and All Angels was on the way to becoming one of the county's wealthier parishes.

This was a considerable relief to me personally. The Wynmore-Russells had been the church's principal benefactor for several generations, as the various commemorative plaques on its walls testified. My wife and I had continued the tradition as far as our means would allow. I wish we could have done more, but our small farm is unprofitable, and my brigadier's pension, though generous, leaves little surplus by the time I have met the alimony obligations from my previous two marriages. We helped the church as best we could, paying for small repairs to the fabric and so forth, but couldn't possibly fund the major maintenance work that was so urgently needed.

All of which should have made me one of Ms Chumleigh's keenest allies. Alas! It did not. Scurrilous rumours said I was upset from the start because she chose to spend her first night in the village at the bar of the Royal Oak rather than coming round to the Hall to talk with the parish's sole remaining church warden and sidesman. That is simply not true. I thought her behaviour strange, perhaps even a little rude, but I did not take umbrage. No, my misgivings ran deeper than mere personal incompatibility.

It began with her dress. I am no prude and have no particular objection to short skirts. On occasion, my own wife and daughters have been known to wear garments that leave little to the imagination. But they are neither in holy orders, nor are they in mourning. We were led to believe that Ms Chumleigh's husband and child perished in a tragic fire just two months before her arrival amongst us.

I do not object to visits to the pub. Some

of my most vivid memories from my time at Sandhurst feature escapades in pubs of one sort or another. But should a Church of England priest stand rounds of drinks for those who are clearly intoxicated? Should they encourage the publican to lock the door and dim the lights so that he can continue serving well after the time permitted by his license? And should they leave so drunk that they have to be escorted back to the rectory by two handsome young men? I think not, Bishop.

Such behaviour may enable the rector to acquire many "fans", who show their loyalty by attending divine service. Nevertheless, I am not sure an intimate hug in the public bar of the Royal Oak or a kiss on the rectory doorstep is an appropriate way to recruit disciples with a sincere faith in Jesus Christ, Our Saviour.

Charisma, like good looks, is a gift God bestows upon certain fortunate individuals. (I am aware that I myself am not one of those so blessed.) It is a talent to be used wisely and for the public good, and not employed for personal gain or aggrandisement. I saw this at first hand in the army. Certain officers, through sheer force of personality, so inspired their men that they would follow them to the ends of the Earth and back. This was fine when the leader was of sound judgement. When they were not, the result could be disastrous.

The charisma of a priest is similarly double-edged. Though its abuse might not bring physical death, it can lead to the far worse fate of spiritual death. I allude to the "primrose path to the everlasting bonfire."

Did Ms Chumleigh employ her obvious charisma to lead her parishioners down that sweet-scented walkway? I fear she did. Through smiles, flattery and gentle gestures, she persuaded traditional churchgoers that her new style of worship – electronic music, hand clasping and a liberal scattering of love (divine and otherwise) – was for the good of the community. Unbelievers found new faith; those who had not been inside the church for years, rediscovered the way to its doors; not one of those who had attended from time to time ceased to do so. All were seduced – I use the word advisedly – by Ms Chumleigh's charm.

At this point I have a confession to make: I too fell under Ms Chumleigh's potent spell. About a fortnight after her arrival, I called on the rectory with a view to offering my resignation as church warden. I did not like way things were going. Specifically, I objected to the appointment of untried and untested teenagers to assist me in my job. I was not keen on their title of "sidespeople", either.

I knocked on the rectory door at around 10 o'clock in the morning, by when I assumed the rector would have breakfasted and started the morning's work. I was mistaken. When my first knock evoked no reply, I tried again. The window above me opened and Ms Chumleigh asked me to "hang on a mo" as she was not yet dressed.

I duly hung on until Ms Chumleigh opened the front door. To my astonishment, I found that she still had not dressed, but had wrapped herself in some sort of oriental-style dressing gown. Her long black hair hung loose over her shoulders. When I offered to come back later, she told me not to be silly and invited me into the kitchen for a cup of coffee. I accepted her invitation and, when she had served the drink, explained the purpose of my visit.

Before I had finished, her eyes had filled with tears and she started to sob. Did I not realise, she asked, dabbing at her eyes with the hem of her gown, that I was the pillar, the rock on which she was rebuilding the church? St Michael and All Angels needed me, the community needed me, she needed me. Her sobs grew louder.

I was the one strong man in the village, she assured me. The Christian soldier – *her* Christian soldier. At this point, she began to plead. Please, please would I remain as warden? Still weeping, she leaned forward and threw her arms around my neck. Please?

It is not necessary for me to say what happened next. Suffice it to say, Bishop, I fell. I remain deeply ashamed and embarrassed by the incident, though I would add that it was but a single lapse. After that grey Monday morning in February, Ms Chumleigh and I maintained a wholly professional relationship.

By then, of course, it was too late. I was completely under her thumb. Thenceforward, she had only to raise an eyebrow to remind me of what, at the time, she had called "our naughty little secret". Had word ever leaked out of what had passed between us, my reputation, my marriage, and my life in Lower Tangthorpe would have lain in tatters. At the age of fifty-five, I was in no position to start all over again. I was trapped.

I could not object when, to clear a space for dancing, the church's ancient wooden pews were removed and either sold or thrown on a huge bonfire in the churchyard. (Ms Chumleigh delighted in fires.) I held my tongue when a team of young volunteers painted the interior walls of the church in a rainbow of pastel pinks, blues and yellows. What could I do when the radical rector was elected to replace me as chair of the village fête committee? I then meekly accepted the unanimous vote to give the proceeds from the next three fêtes towards the "refurbishment and modernization of the church in order to make it the true heart of the village."

I had not felt so impotent since the time when my company was forbidden to retaliate against a stone-throwing Republican mob on the streets of Belfast. I seethed with inner fury.

All of which brings me to the crucial matter at the heart of this report: heating. Ms Chumleigh identified this as an issue of major importance the moment she set foot inside our damp and freezing church. By the end of the month, it had become an obsession, an issue towering over all others. Why that was, I leave it to you, Bishop, to decide. I will limit my contribution to setting forth the evidence as clearly and objectively as I can.

From the outset, Ms Chumleigh decided that the only suitable heating system for St Michael and All Angels would be a ground-source heat pump. Essentially, the device brings thermal energy from deep below the surface and uses it to provide heating and hot water. The rector pointed out, perfectly correctly, that heat pumps were both environmentally friendly and very cheap to run. What she dismissed with a cheerful "where there's a will there's a way" was the enormous cost of installation.

A Parish Ground-Source Heat Pump Committee (PGSHPC) was established with Ms Chumleigh in the chair. She invited me to be its honorary president because, I imagine, she wanted my name on the letterhead. Until then, I had flattered myself that the manner in which she had recruited me to her fan club might have been influenced by attraction. When she informed me that I would "of course" agree to presiding over what she jokingly referred to as her "Hellfire Club", I realised how foolishly mistaken I had been.

My wife and I launched the fundraising campaign with a cheque for £3,000 – a sum we could ill afford. Other donations, promises and bequests followed. Various events, from raffles to "open garden" days, raised further funds, and the church's bank agreed a substantial loan. By the end of June, sufficient money had been raised and the rector set to work. She drew up plans in conjunction with a firm of local architects with experience in adapting listed buildings in a manner acceptable to the authorities. Several quotes were received from installers of ground source heat systems, and a preferred candidate chosen.

Once again, I venture into delicate territory. What I am about to write is hearsay, and perhaps even libellous, yet it accords so closely with the known facts that I feel it my duty to set it down. The borehole required for an effective ground-source heat pump needs to descend to about 100 metres. In unusual circumstances, it may go down to 150 metres, but never further. Being a practical man, I took a keen interest in the technology and made daily visits to observe the work in progress. When the drill had reached 95 metres, the foreman informed me that the geology and temperatures at that depth would be sufficient for the mechanism to work effectively. He planned to stop drilling and move on to installing the surface equipment.

Imagine my surprise, therefore, when the next day I found the drilling had restarted. The site foreman told me, somewhat sheepishly, that it was the rector's idea: she had implored him to drill deeper. This answer drew half-concealed smirks from the other men on site. And so it went on. The drilling continued day after day, deeper and deeper, hotter and hotter. Eventually, I asked one of the workmen to tell me what was going on. "Better ask the governor," he had said, nodding towards the church door.

At that moment, Ms Chumleigh and the foreman appeared, the former beaming beneficently, the latter doing up his hi-vis jacket. My respect for our rector plumbed new depths.

But why, I asked myself as I walked home, did that scandalous woman need to go down so deep? It wasn't necessary. It simply did not make sense.

The drilling eventually stopped at around 250 metres. Over the summer, the pump and other machinery were installed in a carefully concealed underground chamber above the borehole. Inside the church, slim, stone-coloured radiators and unobtrusive pipework replaced the cast-iron fittings generously paid for by my great-grandfather in 1920. By early September, the new system had been tested and found to work perfectly. Only a little cosmetic work remained to be done before the grand opening on Sunday 18th September.

As is my custom, two days ago I wandered down to the church at dusk to check the doors were locked and the remaining builders' equipment secure from thieves. To my surprise, I saw a lone figure standing amid the graves. I approached cautiously, not wishing to disturb a moment of private prayer. As I did so, the figure began to chant. It was an eerie, mystical sound and the words were equally unfamiliar.

I stood still for a moment, trying to make sense of what was being said. I must have moved slightly, for the figure sensed my presence. It hesitated for a second before advancing slowly out of the shadows. 'Brigadier! What a surprise!' It was Ms Chumleigh.

After exchanging a few pleasantries, I asked her what she was doing. She appeared momentarily lost for words and glanced anxiously at the surrounding tombs. As her eye fell upon one of them, she relaxed, and an almost beatific smile spread across her face. She had been praying, she said, for the soul of a young girl buried in the churchyard. Such a tragic story, she sighed, pointing to the gravestone.

It was getting dark, and for someone whose eyes are past their best the name was difficult to read. I bent down and switched on my phone. *Lucie Fernandez, 1845–1857*. Only when I got home and was seated before the television news with a glass of whisky did it dawn on me what Ms Chumleigh had been chanting. She may have been thinking of the maiden buried at her feet, but she had intoned only the first three syllables of the girl's name.

My mind went back to the sermon Ms Chumleigh had preached at matins the previous Sunday. The text, which I'm afraid I don't recall, was taken from John Milton's masterpiece *Paradise Lost*. It was something to do with Satan (whom she called Lucifer) being the most beautiful of all the angels before God threw him out of Heaven. She was a most effective orator and the congregation hung on her every word. However, as I listened to those honeyed syllables, I was gripped by mounting anxiety as she advanced skilfully onto what was, theologically speaking, very thin ice.

She began with the Garden of Eden, God's perfect world. It was ruined, she explained, by the Old Testament prophets. Those "grumpy old misogynists" had two fears. The first was children being born to single mothers without the means to support them. This was perfectly understandable in a "tent-and-desert" society. The "bearded killjoys'" second fear was less rational. They were afraid of women: afraid of being "swallowed up" by women's bodies, afraid because women were more intelligent than them, and afraid because women were psychologically the stronger and more resilient gender.

Driven by these two fears, "Moses & Co" constructed the "the great lie": women were weaker than men, sex was sin, and where men and women erred from the straight and narrow, it was always the woman's fault. And the whole wicked system was held in place by physical force – the only area in which male superiority was undeniable.

And what did Ms Chumleigh conclude from this heretical diatribe? Many attributes of the so-called "God" were false: He was love, physical as well as spiritual and emotional. As such, He could not be jealous or judging or cruel. Only a twisted mind could dream up the myth of "free will". The deity created by old men long ago was a tyrant, just as they themselves were tyrants.

According to Ms Chumleigh, the snake had entered the Garden of Eden to remind Adam and Eve of love's pure joy, to free them from the despot god. That's why Satan or "the Devil" is also known as "Lucifer", a name that means "light bearer". It was the Romans' name for Venus, the morning star and goddess of love.

By this point, Bishop, I was clenching my fists, fighting to stop myself shouting out at the lies the fiendish woman was spreading in the name of Christianity. Looking around me, I saw I was alone in my fury. Every other member of the congregation, old and young, male and female, was transfixed by the mesmerising rhetoric.

I should have interrupted, I know. But I was too cowardly, terrified lest Ms Chumleigh reveal "our naughty little secret" there and then, before the whole village. I bit my tongue and sat in shameful silence as the sermon came to its hideously ominous conclusion. Lucifer was not God's enemy. He was part of God, the original God that those grim old Israelites had twisted beyond recognition. Hell was not a place of torment but warm and kindly. Its fire – the fire that would soon warm our church – was pure and bright and godly.

I should have reported Ms Chumleigh to the church authorities that very morning. But I did not. I should have challenged her when she was chanting over the grave of Lucie Fernandez. But I did not. For reasons I have explained, I put my own preservation above that of the church.

And now it is too late.

At about 3.30 am on the day after my churchyard meeting with Ms Chumleigh, I was woken by the sound of fire engines. The telephone rang five minutes later. It was the police, informing me of a serious fire in the church. I dressed hastily and hurried into the village to see what was going on.

Though I have seen action in several war zones, including Iraq, I do not believe I ever encountered a sight quite like that which met my eyes as I turned the corner by the Royal Oak. Even from over a quarter of a mile away, it was clear that the blaze was extremely serious. It must have started around midnight, for it had gutted the ancient building long before the emergency services arrived.

St Michael and all Angels was roaring like a furnace from which a pall of thick grey smoke rose to obscure the stars overhead. All combustible furniture and fittings were gone, and the medieval oak of the roof timbers had collapsed. As the heat melted their leaden binding, the beautiful stained-glass windows, once the pride of the diocese, had fallen to pieces like broken jigsaw puzzles. It was an appalling sight.

However, it was not so much the ferocity of the blaze that held the assembled crowd of villagers spellbound as their shape. There appeared to be two fires. One was the conflagration destroying the church building; the other, right next to it, was a pillar of flame, like a gigantic firework, rising 100 metres or more into the night sky. The source of this extraordinary volcano, clearly visible now everything around it had been burned or blasted away, was the gaping mouth of the borehole.

I approached the firefighter in command of the operation. Attempts to extinguish the flames were futile, he exclaimed. As soon as they managed to dampen down the fire in the church, the heat from the column of fire reignited it. He had never seen the like. It was, he said, as if someone had "opened the gates of hell".

Just when we feared the fire might never be extinguished, something extraordinary happened. By half past six the sky was lightening noticeably, and at 6.51 the first rays of the sun appeared across the fields to our right. At that moment – at that precise moment – the fiery pillar died back into the horrible black hole from which it had erupted, and a chilling silence descended like a snowfall over the scene.

The firefighters, the police, and the crowd of onlookers stared in disbelief at the cracked stones and charred timbers beside that ghastly pit. Their faces, mine included, were blank with incomprehension, for we had all witnessed something truly terrible.

Experts, seeking a scientific explanation for the disaster, are already talking of fracking damage and a rare geological fault. As I know – and now you, Bishop – their efforts to apply the laws of natural science to the unnatural are in vain. Unfortunately, I am unable to get hold of the one person who might confirm this.

For the past two days the Lower Tangthorpe rectory has stood empty. Its former incumbent, the Rev Mary Chumleigh, was last seen watching the fire beside the grave of Lucie Fernandez. Since then, she has completely disappeared.

Yours faithfully,

Timothy Wynmore-Russell, DSO

Drone

'Drone? What do you mean, Ali? What drone?'

Alicia sat on the edge of her bed and raised her open palms on either side of her face, like shields. 'I'm sorry, Tom. I don't mean drone.'

'So, what *do* you mean? Come on, this isn't you.'

'I know, I know!' she said, rocking backwards and forwards like a creature in a cage. 'I just *can't* go.' Her tone was desperate, as if she knew what she ought to do but could bring herself to do it.

Tom was trying not to get irritated. 'Look, I don't get it, Ali. Nor does Russ. Have you suddenly gone off him? Has he said something, done something?'

Alicia bowed her head and stared at the floor.

'No, of course not. You know I really like him.'

'Then for God's sake give us a *reason*!'

'Alright. I'm scared.'

It was Alicia's birthday. She and Russell Lozowski had been going out for almost a year now, and for over a week he'd been preparing a special birthday dinner for her in his room: he'd sent her a hand-written invitation, bought scented candles and proper wine glasses, and ordered a posh delivery service, including champagne, that had cost more than he normally spent on food in a month.

At five-thirty, two hours before she was expected, Ali had called to say she had to stay in her hall of residence. She couldn't tell Russell why – not on the phone, anyway. If he came over, she'd try to explain.

Confused and disappointed, Russell said there was no way he was going to cancel. He couldn't come over now because he had last-minute preparations to finish and needed to be in his room when the food and drink arrived. In the end, after another fruitless phone call, he'd sent his best mate Tom round to Alicia's to see what she was up to.

As he made his way across the campus, Tom heard a swishing sound overhead. Looking up at a large drone, and assuming it was one of those the BBC was using to make a film of uni life, he grinned and gave it a little wave. *Must remember to tell Mum to look out for me when she watches the programme.*

Tom had found Alicia close to tears. In response to his questions, she promised it had nothing to do with Russ or her family or her work or any of her friends. All she would say was that she couldn't – daren't – leave the building.

'You said "drone" when I came in,' said Tom. 'You're not afraid of that thing the BBC's using, are you?'

She lifted her head and stared at him. 'What thing?'

'The camera drone videoing the campus. I saw it on my way over. Big, noisy bastard.'

'You've seen it?'

'Yeah. I just told you.'

She took a deep breath and brushed her long black hair off her face. 'You won't believe me, Tom.'

'Try me.'

'I've never told anyone this.' She bit her bottom lip and looked down again. 'You see … that thing out there … it's … it's not a drone.'

'Eh?'

'I said you wouldn't believe me,' she cried, jumping to her feet and knocking over the birthday cards on her bedside locker. 'I knew I shouldn't have told you.' She sniffed and, with the back of her hand, wiped away the tears running down her cheeks.

Tom put a hand on her shoulder. 'I didn't say I

didn't believe you, Ali. Come on. You've got this far, so sit down and explain. If that thing's not a drone, what is it?'

She sat and picked up the fallen cards in silence. When they were back in place, she turned and stared at him. 'Promise not to laugh?'

'Promise.'

'And promise you won't go back to Russ and tell him I'm an idiot?'

'Promise.'

She glanced anxiously out of the window, 'Is it still there?'

Tom stood up and looked outside. 'Can't see it.'

She sighed. 'Good. Well, listen. No interruptions and no judgements, okay?'

'I'm all yours, Ali. Shoot …'

Inspired by a visit to the ancient city of Mohenjodaro when they were children, Alicia and her elder brother Nehal had both chosen to study archaeology at university. They were particularly interested in trade links between the early civilizations of the Indus Valley with those of Mesopotamia and Egypt, and hoped one day to research the topic at postgraduate level.

Nehal got a first-class degree and started on a

Masters in the archaeology of the Near East. As part of the programme, he had an opportunity to go on a dig near St Catherine, close to the famous Mount Sinai in Egypt's Negev Desert. The area fascinated him. As well as being of great historical and theological significance, it was also steeped in ancient myth and legend.

When Alicia heard what her brother was doing, she asked if she'd be allowed to join the expedition. Nehal's tutor ummed and ahed before eventually agreeing – as long as she paid her way. Alicia's mother, saying it would be good for her daughter not to spend the whole summer "entwined with Russell", duly paid up.

A couple of weeks scratching around the ruins of what was thought to have been an ancient Jewish temple produced nothing of much interest or significance. After long days out under a blazing sun, in the evenings the more sociable members of the group piled into their hired Jeep and took themselves off to St Catherine for a few cool beers. Nehal and Alicia, always keen for a bit of fun, were regulars on the Jeep run, and Nehal often brought a few beers home in a cool box to finish the party round a brushwood fire back at their camp.

Then, at the beginning of the third week, the party made a truly significant find. Surprisingly, the discovery was Alicia's. Scraping away the sand from a wall that had collapsed over two millennia ago, she noticed that one of the stones was carved. Carefully, one small area at a time, she brushed off the dusty covering to reveal the design. It was not a building block but a small head-and-shoulders statue, about a metre tall.

An eye – part-human, part-insect – stared up at her. She swept away another few centimetres, and a second eye appeared. No nose – the image certainly wasn't human – and sunken cheeks on a long, narrow, goat-like face. Beneath the eyes lay a thin-lipped mouth, a sort of sideways beak. Alicia said it looked like the powerful mouth of a squid or octopus.

The head was attached to a leathery chest by a thin, ribbed neck like ET's or the expandable hose on a vacuum cleaner. The background was intriguing. At first, Alicia thought it was some sort of gauze curtain but on closer examination she realised it was wings – this mysterious creature could fly!

She turned back to the lidless eyes. The sculptor had clearly taken great pains to get them exactly as he wanted: staring, unblinking, nasty. No, she thought, not just nasty. Evil.

Despite the heat of the day, she shivered. Telling herself not to be so stupid, she stood up, brushed the dirt off her knees, and hurried off to tell the others what she had found.

Dr Ahmed Mustafa, the leader of the dig, was fascinated. After a preliminary examination, he decided the image was one of the very few ancient representations of Beelzebub. The name, he explained to Alicia and Nehal, derived from "Baal" and "zebub". Baal, meaning "lord" was an ancient god of the Canaanites, and the onomatopoeic zebub meant a fly. The two together – "Beelzebub" – had been variously interpreted as "Lord of the Flies" (as in William Golding's famous novel) or "Lord of the Fliers".

By Christian times, Mustafa continued, Beelzebub had morphed into some sort of demon, one of the seven Princes of Hell. His name frequently cropped up in the infamous Salem witch trials, and some believed he was Satan himself.

At this point, his explanation was interrupted by a commotion near the stores tent. The expedition's deputy leader, Dr Levison, was having a furious argument with the driver, cook and two general helpers they had hired in Sharm El-Sheikh. All four were sitting in the Jeep with their baggage, clearly ready to depart and leave the rest of the party stranded in the desert.

The problem was the Beelzebub statue. Mustafa and Levison had asked the workmen to crate it up so it could be taken back to Cairo for proper examination. As soon as the men saw it, they had backed away in terror. Did the scientists not realise what they had done? They had unearthed the Devil! Satan lived in his representations, which was partly why Islam banned the making of all images. If the scientists would not replace the statue exactly as it had been found, buried in the ground, the men would leave immediately.

Faced with the prospect of having to abandon the dig entirely, Mustafa agreed to the men's demands. In the morning, he told them, his team would dig a deep pit and lay the statue to rest within it. Before that, would he be allowed to measure and photograph it? The men agreed, as long as they were not involved. Later, Mustafa confided in Nehal that he hoped to return with a less superstitious team to dig up the statue and take it to Cairo, as originally planned. He had no time for medieval superstitions about stone Satans.

Nor had Nehal. That evening, seated at the bar of the St Catherine Plaza Hotel, he gave vent to his feelings. He couldn't believe that, in the 21st century, a handful of credulous workmen – pedlars of "Neanderthal mumbo-jumbo" – could have stymied important academic research by an act of crude blackmail.

Alicia shared his frustration. Nevertheless, glancing around at the scowls of some of the other customers, she advised Nehal not to trumpet his opinion too loudly in public. They could have a good old moan together when they were alone. The barman, who had been pretending not to listen, nodded in agreement, and Nehal kept his opinions to himself until they returned to camp.

Once they had zipped up their shared tent and cracked open the Heineken six-pack they'd brought back, brother and sister let rip. They began by discussing Dr Mustafa's decision to rebury the statue. Okay, Nehal admitted, he had no choice. But he could at least have tried to explain to the recalcitrant workmen that their fears were outdated nonsense.

'Dr Mustafa's crash course in secularism – free to all believers!' giggled Alicia.

After that, as the first can made way for the second, their talk became more flippant. 'Satan and Baba Yaga held on fraud charges,' quipped Nehal. 'Headlines in *The Sun*.'

'Both held on Baal,' added Alicia.

Ten minutes later, as Nehal emptied a third can, he lay back and closed his eyes. 'Apart from this bloody desert, Ali, the only place where Satan can make a living nowadays is Hollywood!'

'Wrong, Nehal! There's a big demand for him at Halloween.'

He laughed. 'How about hiring out your Beelzebub for a trick or treat, eh?'

Alicia remembered how she had felt when she first uncovered it. 'Yeah, it really *is* quite scary looking.'

'So's the Chamber of Horrors in Madame Tussaud's,' retorted Nehal. 'Scary looks never hurt anyone. That Beelzebub guy's not going to jump up and bite my dick off if I piss all over him, is he?'

'One in the eye for Beelzebub,' Alicia giggled. She paused for a moment. 'You wouldn't, would you?'

'Wouldn't what?'

'Piss on it.'

'I bloody would!'

And so, as his sister held a torch to make sure he was on target, the drunken Nehal Jivraj urinated onto the face of Beelzebub.

Having staggered back to their tent, brother and sister lay side by side in silence, ashamed of what they had done. They had been guilty of a double desecration. To those for whom the statue had religious significance, its despoliation was blasphemy; for an archaeologist to spray a precious artifact with urine was, from a scientific point of view, equally sacrilegious.

Before they fell asleep, they agreed to keep the whole foolish business to themselves. It was only a drunken student prank, wasn't it? They were greatly relieved the following morning to find the statue dry and unmarked. No one need ever know what had happened.

The stone Beelzebub was reburied, as Mustafa had promised, and the rest of the dig passed without incident. At the end of the fifth week, the camp was packed up, loaded onto a truck, and taken back to Sharm Al-Sheikh. The students and their mentors followed in the Jeep.

As a reward for all their hard work, Dr Mustafa had arranged a night of luxury in the Lido Sharm Hotel before they flew back to the UK. Nehal and Alicia swam in the beautiful rooftop pool, enjoyed their first well-cooked meal for over a month, and returned to the moonlit roof to gaze out over the glittering lights of the resort.

Shortly before midnight, Alicia's phone rang. It was Russell. There had been no coverage in the desert, and this was the first time he'd been able to get hold of her. Wanting a bit of privacy, she wandered off to sit behind one of the decorative palms that adorned the far end of the terrace.

Ten minutes later, after a happy but very expensive chat, she returned to find Nehal lying beside the pool. He was dead.

The post-mortem revealed that he had died of a catastrophic brain haemorrhage. The specialist explained to a weeping Alicia that some people were born with a congenital weakness in a cerebral artery. It only became apparent – too late – when the subject experienced a sudden trauma, such as a fall.

Her brother may have stumbled over a chair in

the darkness and knocked his head as he fell. As there was no cut or bruising, however, the fall itself may have triggered the haemorrhage.

Alicia nodded. Could something non-physical, like being startled by a sound or sight, have the same effect? she asked

The doctor thought for a moment. It was possible, he said, but extremely rare. He had heard of cases where seeing an unpleasant event, like a mugging, caused a sufficiently dramatic rise in blood pressure to trigger a cerebral bleed. Her brother had experienced no such shock, had he?

Alicia shook her head. No, not that she knew of. Not that she'd tell a science-trained doctor, anyway. She wasn't going to risk being laughed at or patronised.

While talking to Russell, she had heard something. It was a sort of whirring noise above the roof of the hotel. At first, she thought it was a drone. Then, as it approached, she realized it was more like the beating of wings.

She recalled the horrified look on Nehal's face when she found him, too. It was not the expression of someone who had simply tripped over.

Wondering about the strange noise, she

glanced up at the night sky. A dark object, like a huge insect, passed across the face of the moon and disappear into the night. The shape of the wings looked familiar, though at the time she couldn't remember why.

'When I had time to think, I realized what it was,' said Alicia, looking carefully at Tom to see how he had reacted to her story. 'It was Beelzebub, of course.'

Tom adopted his "I am not judging you" expression.

'He'd come to take his revenge, hadn't he?' Alicia continued, her fingers twisting like the tentacles of a sea anemone. 'But he'd only got half of it.'

'What do you mean?'

'I'm still here. After Nehal died and I was unharmed, I thought I was ok. After all, I'd only held the torch.

'I now realize it hasn't forgotten. It's been looking for me all this time, and now it's found me, it's going to kill me. I know it is, Tom.'

Tom took a deep breath. 'Right,' he began slowly, 'let's take this thing step by step. First, whatever happened to your brother was really tragic, and I'm very, very sorry.'

'Thanks, Tom. I'm getting over it, slowly. I don't think mum and dad ever will. Obviously, I haven't been able to talk to them about what happened, what *really* happened.'

'No, of course not. His official cause of death was brain haemorrhage, right?'

'Yes but – '

'Leave the "but" for the moment, Ali. The doctor said he fell over and may have banged his head – '

'He hadn't seen the look on Nehal's face.'

'True.'

'Nor heard the noise.'

'True again. But you must admit it's possible – only possible, mind you – that the flapping sound you heard was a bird, or even a drone. Nehal tripped over because he was looking at it.'

'That's not what happened, Tom.'

'But it is possible, yes?'

'To you, yes. Not to me.'

Tom nodded. 'Alright. Here's another possibility: the BBC are using a large drone to film the campus, so that could have been what you saw and heard out there?'

A resigned look came over Alicia's face. 'I know where you're going, Tom. You think I've made the whole thing up.'

'No, I don't, Ali.' Tom placed the tips of his fingers together, as if their symmetrical pattern somehow represented the logic of his argument. 'All I'm saying is that there are alternative explanations. And, if we're honest, more rational ones. Don't you reckon that if there really was some sort of devil thing flying about looking for you, someone – air traffic control, for example – would have picked it up by now?'

'Maybe.'

Tom relaxed. For the first time, Alicia seemed to accept that her fears might be mistaken. He pressed home his advantage. 'And if this flying devil's so amazing, why has it taken him almost a year to find you?' 'I don't know.'

'Nor do I, Ali. It doesn't make sense, does it?'

The conversation continued for another threequarters of an hour. Gradually, point by point, Tom persuaded Alicia that her anxiety was based on a series of coincidences. The stone statue was cleverly carved, yes, but it was no more dangerous than the walking mummies in Hammer Horror movies. Nehal died after he tripped over a chair in the dark and banged his head, not because he was scared out of his wits by a flying demon. And the thing buzzing about outside was making a TV programme, not looking for someone who had held a torch while her brother pissed on it.

When Tom finally called Russell to say that Ali would be over around 7.30 as planned, she looked like someone who had woken from a nightmare, her face shining with relief and happiness.

'Sorry, Tom,' she said as he left. 'I've been a bloody fool, haven't I? I can't tell you how much you've helped – the whole thing had been gnawing away at me ever since Nehal died. I got things all out of proportion, didn't I?'

'It was perfectly understandable after what you'd been through.'

'Beelzebub, eh? Doh!' She banged a fist on her forehead in a parody of Homer Simpson.

They laughed, gave each other a hug, and Tom went back to his room to finish an essay due the next morning. He had reached the bottom of page three and was in the middle of googling how to reference an article, when the phone rang. It was Russell.

'She hasn't turned up, Tom.'

'Shit! She must have got cold feet at the last minute. Leave it with me, Russ. I'll go over there now.'

His path lay across a grass park dotted with ancient oaks and beeches that had stood there long before the university was built. Between two of these trees, about 100 metres from Alicia's hall, a small crowd had gathered in the pale evening light. Tom broke into a trot. *What the hell …?*

As he grew nearer, he found he was crossing himself, something he had not done since he renounced his Christian upbringing eight years previously. 'Jesus Christ!' he muttered. 'Jesus Christ! Jesus Christ!'

Some of the crowd were crying. A couple with basic first aid training knelt beside Alicia's body, unsure what to do. No one had prepared them for a severed carotid artery. So much blood.

From far away came the sound of an ambulance siren. Tom pushed to the front of the crowd. 'Did anyone see what happened?'

'I heard a scream,' sobbed the woman beside him. 'I ran over. By the time I got here, she was dead.'

'Hear anything else? A drone?'

The woman shook her head. 'Not really. Just a sort of flapping.'

Speed Cameras

I run my hand gently across the smooth of her waist and down to her thigh.

'My God, Marta, do you really exist?'

'I hope so. I feel solid enough, don't I?' She guides my hand lower.

I lean over and kiss her eyelids. 'I mean, how can anyone be so lovely? You're way too beautiful for this world.'

She raises her right leg so it lies over mine and smiles. 'You're right, Leon. I'm from another world. I materialise from a parallel universe the second you take my clothes off. Flash! A different me.'

Though we first dated three years ago and have now been married for eight months, we have never been closer, more in love.

'You are my only universe,' I whisper, my lips brushing against her ear.

'That's nice.' She makes a purring noise. 'But maybe we're in two cars in separate lanes of the same motorway, moving in parallel? Like this.' She presses against me so our bodies are touching all the way down, toe to breast. 'I'm in one lane and you're in the other.'

Finding the image strangely disconcerting, I make light of it. 'When I look out of the car window,' I say, gazing into her infinite eyes, 'I see a luscious little alien looking back at me.'

'Lucky you! But what if you're the alien and I'm real?'

I laugh. 'Then you're in bed with an alien.'

'Uh-huh. Never one of my fantasies.' She nibbles at my lips like a rabbit. 'Actually, I think we're in the same universe, my darling, not in parallel ones.' 'How do you know?'

'Because we're touching.' She moves her hips.

'You know how our universe was made?'

'With a flash?'

'No, with a Big Bang.'

'Ah yes, I remember.' I kiss her bare shoulder. 'Shall we make another universe …?'

It's a special night, a time of wine and love-making to make the beginning of our separation more bearable. There are moments when it feels like a wake.

From tomorrow morning, we'll be apart for three weeks. Three whole weeks! For the first time since we met, I'll spend a night alone.

Marta is flying to Australia to visit her mother who has been diagnosed with breast cancer. The oncologist assures her that it was diagnosed early and that she will make a full recovery. Even so, as an only child Marta feels duty bound to be with her mother at this worrying time. Besides, though she knows her father is doing his best, Aussie cattle ranchers are not the planet's most sensitive creatures.

What am I going to do while she's away? The thought of coming home every evening to an empty house is too depressing. Her clothes in the bedroom, her toiletries in the bathroom, her boots by the back door, her little notes to me in the kitchen, her scent lingering throughout the house … No, that would be how it is when your partner dies suddenly, like my grandfather felt when Grandma had a fatal stroke at the age of fifty-six.

Home without Marta would be no home at all.

I have signed up for the first session of the company's residential management course in Newcastle University. The dates coincide almost exactly: Marta leaves tomorrow, Sunday 3rd, and returns on the morning of Saturday 24th. My course finishes on the previous Thursday, giving me time to get home and prepare the nest for my angel's return.

Though they say parting is sweet sorrow, that's only half of it. As Marta and I wrap our arms round each other, we present an image of unspoken emotion flowing between us, like electricity. The reality's a bit different. Our minds are already one step ahead, hers hoping she's remembered to pack everything she needs, mine to the long drive north and the forthcoming course.

We don't say much. After we've repeated for the tenth time how much we love each other and she's driven off, I return to the house and pack my own things. I call her twice before she reaches the airport, and she calls me after she's passed through passports and security. Beyond the barrier.

The journey to Newcastle takes six hours. I play music and focus on what to expect from the course. The subject is "Modern management: handling a workforce working from home", and I think up a few questions that

I hope will sound intelligent like, "How do you check an employee's working hours?" and "What household expenses can they offset against tax?"

Around Cambridge, I wonder what Marta is doing at this moment. Eating? Sleeping? Watching a movie …?

A lorry with Romanian plates pulls out in front of me, forcing me to brake suddenly. As I do so, I notice the car on my left and am reminded of Marta's words from the previous night: "two cars in different lanes of the same motorway, moving in parallel."

Strange for this to be happening now, just as we are having to live separate lives for the first time.

I glance in my mirrors to see if I can pull out. No, a silver-grey BMW is coming up fast in the outside lane and I fall in behind the lorry again. The car to my left is still there, exactly level, precisely the same speed. I check out the driver.

Uncanny. She has Marta's profile, the same brown hair cut short in the style of a 60s pop singer, the same fashionable glasses, the same … I check on the lorry once more. It's swaying slightly as it struggles to get ahead of a car transporter. *At this rate, we'll be here all bloody day!*

Is my doppelganger travelling companion thinking the same thing? I turn towards her. She does the same and we smile as our eyes meet. It can't be Marta, and yet ...

The car behind flashes its headlights. The Romanian lorry has finished its manoeuvre and pulled in, leaving me blocking the lane. I acknowledge my fault with a wave to the car on my tail and accelerate away.

For a moment I'm tempted to slow down and see if the Marta look-alike catches me up, but the voice of reason dissuades me. *Don't be so bloody daft, Leon! Get a grip! It's all in the imagination. There must be a million women who look a bit like Marta. Besides, you know she's on a plane at 30,000 feet over Indonesia. You're tired. Take a break and grab a coffee.* I do precisely that.

My time in Newcastle passes quicker than I expect. My room is small but clean and comfortable. The course is well organised and at the weekends I'm free to explore the beautiful, desolate Northumbrian coastline. On the second Sunday I drive up to Lindisfarne, the Holy Island, and stand among the red stone ruins of the ancient abbey.

Apparently, the place was founded by an Irishman named Aiden, who's now a saint. I ask the guide by the door what a saint is, and she says it's a very holy person who has performed miracles or had miracles performed in their name.

Miracles, like magic? I ask. She looks at me suspiciously. No, not like magic, she replies. Miracles reflect the power of God in the world.

I'm no wiser, but our brief conversation takes me back to what Marta had said: "I materialise from a parallel universe the second you take my clothes off. Flash! A different me."

Maybe that's what those Aiden-types were on about, except they used the vocabulary of religion instead of science? Did they know instinctively that there were laws beyond those of physics and chemistry? St Marta – why not? The idea makes me smile as I buy an ice-cream and wend my way slowly back to the car. Only three hours before my next Skype with Australia.

The daily chats (occasionally with extravagant virtual sex when her mother isn't around) are the focal point of my day. We don't talk about much – I offer some detail of the day's seminar or role play, she relates an experience in the local supermarket or something her parents have said – and an hour or two slips by without either of us noticing.

When I mention her doppelganger in the car

beside me on the motorway, she laughs. 'That must be the other me. The one in the next-door universe.'

On my return from Lindisfarne, I tell her she's been made a saint. 'Thanks, Leon,' she says, 'but I thought they were all supposed to be virgins?'

'No, all they have to do is perform miracles.'

'Can I do that?'

'Sure. Your very existence is a miracle to me.'

'Yuk! You're drifting off into the other lane again.'

'As long as you're there too, I don't care. I love you, Marta. Have I ever told you that?'

'Er, I don't think so. Whatever, I love you too, Leon. From your tufty hair and green eyes to your lovely loins and pointy toes – all mine in a few short days.'

'I can't wait!'

'Neither can I, my darling. Neither can I.'

It's early evening by the time I've filled in the course evaluation form, said my goodbyes, and set out for home. Having come up on the M1, I take the A1 back south. It's longer, but the old road's countless roundabouts and shabby petrol stations make a change from the monotonous uniformity of the motorway.

There are speed cameras, too. I first encounter one when it flashes a Range Rover heading north near Newark. More flashes just after Grantham and outside Peterborough. I find them unsettling, not because I'm speeding – the limiter takes care of that – but because … Actually, I'm not too sure why. It's something to do with the sudden brilliance in the fading evening light. It's shocking. Like an eerie sign from another world more powerful than ours.

I wish Marta was with me.

It's past midnight when I arrive home and collapse into bed. At breakfast the following morning, I plough through the mail. Eighty per cent junk, a couple of bills, a reminder from the dentist and a formal-looking envelope with my name and address showing through a transparent plastic window.

Bloody hell! It's a speeding ticket. I check the car registration – mine. But the time and place? Ridiculous! How could I possibly have been doing 41 mph on Market Hill at 10.42 am on Wednesday 13 August when at the time I was sitting in

Seminar Room 12 discussing what time one could reasonably expect an employee working from home to take a work-related phone call.

I add "Police Station" beneath "flower shop", "off-licence" and "supermarket" on the list of places I have to visit this morning. I then circle it with an arrow pointing to the top of the list. I want to get the stupid business out of the way before I do anything else.

The Traffic Law Infringement Disputes Officer is a young woman with fair hair. I compare her unfavourably with Marta. When she announces herself as "Dawn Perkins", my inappropriate remark about a false dawn is not well received. Things have got off to a bad start.

They get worse when she produces a photograph of my car on Market Hill. The time and date, recorded in white lettering on the bottom right of the picture, are the same as those on my penalty notice. The speed readout is printed bottom left – 41 mph.

The information appears beyond dispute, but that does not concern me. My eyes are fixed on the face of the man driving the car. It's not too clear because the light from the flash is reflecting off the windscreen. Even so, the figure at the wheel looks very much like me. Impossible. But …

'It does look like you, sir,' says Dawn.

'I agree. But it couldn't be.'

'Do you deny that you were driving the car?'

'Of course I do! I was in Newcastle.'

Dawn nods. She's obviously heard this sort of thing a dozen times before, and she's learned her response by heart. 'If you can produce incontrovertible evidence of that, sir, we will investigate further. Without it, I'm afraid we have no alternative but to support the charge.'

I say I'll return on Monday with sworn testimony supporting my presence in Newcastle at the time of the offence. Dawn says she doesn't work Mondays. Her place on Disputes will be taken by Sergeant Gerry Coaller, and she'll be handing the case on to him.

By the time I've left the police station and walked the half mile to the off-licence, my annoyance has turned to nagging anxiety. What's happening? A fragment from somewhere in my GCSE Eng Lit syllabus floats into my mind: "nothing is but what is not."

For the second time in recent weeks, I find

myself muttering, 'Get a grip, Leon! Get a grip!' I need Marta back with me more than ever.

Marta calls immediately after her flight has landed. 'With luck, I'll be home in a couple of hours,' she announces. 'Can't wait, sweetheart.' Neither can I.

I check the flowers in the sitting room and beside our bed. My "Welcome Home!" banner in the hall is a bit crooked, so I straighten it. I even give the shower tray another wipe.

Everything has to be perfect.

I stand in the drive and gaze up the road, making a bet with myself: *hers will be the fourth car to appear*. It's the fifth and I hope it's not an omen.

Should I rush up and open the car door for her? No, that'd make me look like some sycophantic creep at a posh hotel. I'll just stand, arms wide, grinning. Welcome back darling!

First, it's the long, loving hug. She smells different, a mixture of Australia and aeroplane. Then it's the kiss, the first kiss for three weeks. Long, lingering, exploring. I have forgotten what she tastes like.

She breaks off and takes a step back, letting go of my hand. 'Leon … You …You've …' I can almost see her brain working. The expression on her face changes from happy confusion to something that's almost fearful.

'Darling, before we go any further, I simply must go to the loo. I'm bursting!'

She brushes past me into the house and heads straight for the bathroom. I follow, smiling. *Of course, meeting after three weeks apart is bound to be a little bit awkward. Things can't possibly be exactly as they were before. She's experienced things, I've experienced things. We have to re-set.*

I'm interrupted by a voice. Her voice. She's talking to someone on her phone. I move closer to the bathroom door and listen. 'Yes, of course it's an emergency. There's an intruder in my house.'

I take a step back, unable to take in what I've just heard. She's still talking. 'Police? Yes … yes … 'Well, for a start he's got different-coloured eyes.'

I'm close to tears. 'Marta! Marta darling, what the hell are you doing?'

She does not reply. I grab the handle and try to open the door.

Locked. Marta has locked me out.

No-brainer

They met in the communal kitchen on day one. Steve was there first, opening a tin of spaghetti. He glanced up but didn't say anything when Eldon breezed in.

'This the kitchen, then?' Eldon was a born icebreaker.

Steve looked up. 'Yeah. That's what it says on the door, anyway.'

They both half-smiled. The ice was broken.

By the time Halila came in, the two boys had swapped course information – Steve, Electrical Engineering; Eldon, Economics – and told each other where they lived.

'Edgbaston, Birmingham,' said Steve. 'Not far from the cricket ground. I've been once or twice with my mum. She loves cricket.'

Eldon laughed. 'Takes all sorts. Wouldn't get my mum there. Leamington – that's quite near you – is where I come from. Dad's a builder.'

Steve stirred the spaghetti into a pan.

'Got his own firm,' Eldon went on. 'Proper jobs, not cowboy stuff. I worked for him in the summer.

Twenty-five quid an hour. Not bad, eh?'

'Way more than me,' said Steve. 'Tesco do the basic.'

Enter Halila.

'Hi,' said Eldon, checking out the thick black hair cut short, the purple lipstick, ripped jeans, and "I LOVE WEIRD" T-shirt. Not for me, he decided. He didn't know how to react to "weird". He liked normal, straightforward girls who smiled at his good looks and laughed at his breezy confidence. He never knew where he was with the weird ones, and he'd never hung around long enough to find out.

The suspicion was mutual. To Halila, the too-clean trainers, freshly close-cropped hair and here-I-am manner signalled straight, basic, normal. Ok, she thought, but not interesting. Probably a notches-on-the-bedpost type. She looked at Steve. So, what about him, the quiet guy cooking something? Unassuming but honest. Domesticated, too. Nice to find one of the boys she'd be sharing with was not an unreconstructed slob. He might be interesting, too. With luck, even a little bit weird?

Weird people interested her. That's why she had rejected her parents' choice of Law or Medicine and opted instead for Sociology with Psychology. When she told them, they threw her out of the house. She packed a bag and left that same evening. In the hall, after she had said goodbye, she asked them to give her best wishes to Uncle Sanjid and thank him for screwing up her life. She slammed the front door behind her before they could reply.

'I'm Steve,' said Steve. 'Got some spaghetti here. You guys want some?' That's how it started.

The first year went as one might have predicted. Steve worked hard, stayed off drugs, met Zoe in the second term and planned to move in with her the following year. Eldon got drunk, brought a string of girls back to his room, was predicted to fail his Economics exams and switched to Tourism in the nick of time. He didn't tell his parents.

Halila did alright at her work, especially the Psychology, but her social life was a bit of a mystery. She dated Steve for a couple of weeks at the end of October. After they'd broken up, Eldon asked his mate what'd gone wrong. Steve didn't say much, only that he felt he was being treated "like a piece of evidence". If that was true, then he must have been the yardstick of "normal" against which Halila measured her other lovers. For Eldon, the procession of heavily tattooed, drug-taking, bi-sexual men and women that traipsed in and out of Halila's room were a "load of fucking nutcases".

The most disturbing story came from Gary, one of Eldon's mates in the football club. He swore he'd seen a girl looking just like Halila with a well-known local addict. A week later, the man was found guilty of strangling his girlfriend and setting fire to her house. No one had any hard evidence for Gary's story – Halila's name did not come up at the trial and she dismissed it as a "load of bullshit". Even so, after a long talk with her tutor at the end of the year, she became more selective over her choice of partners and talked of wanting a First so she could go on to postgraduate research.

'Any idea what subject, like, topic?' Steve had asked.

She gave him a half smile. 'Can't you guess?'

'Weird stuff?'

'Not stuff, Steve. People. Outsiders, the guys you call sickos.'

And that's how they went on. Eldon finally told his parents about his change of course, managed to stay off the booze and women long enough to get a degree, and talked his way into a job with Sky Blue travel agents in Mitcham.

Steve got a First, married Zoe, and got a steady job with a small firm in Brentford making specialist instruments for British Aerospace.

Halila got a First, too, though no one from her family acknowledged it by coming to the award ceremony. Her hair was now dyed blonde and "Weird" was no longer emblazoned across the front of her T-shirt but tattooed in red, green and blue up both arms. Other parts of her body were decorated with similar off-beat words, images and piercings. Her aim of the last two years had not changed: she was set on doing research. Her chosen field was the Sociology of Sociopaths; specifically, as she explained to Eldon, "Whether or not sickos are self-made."

She spent all summer trying to find a supervisor willing to take her on. Despite encouraging responses to her initial emails, none of her eight interviews resulted in an offer. Undaunted, she found a job in Hackney town planning office and carried on her research in the evenings and at weekends.

Which brings us to where we are now: 6 pm in the Prince George, Rochester Street, Clapham.

It's late September, exactly eight years since that first meeting in the shared kitchen at the hall of residence.

It was Steve's idea, or rather Zoe's. She'd just had a get-together with her first-year uni flatmates and suggested he do the same. He wasn't too sure at first. Did he really want to spend an evening listening to Eldon's casual bragging and staring at Halila's confrontational body art? After all, it wasn't as if they'd seen that much of each other after the first year. But Zoe persisted and he decided to give it a go. None of the three had changed their mobile numbers. He was mildly surprised when the others joined his "Drake's Hall Reunion" WhatsApp group, and even more surprised when they said they could make the Prince George on the date and time he'd suggested.

He gets there first, settling himself at a table with a good view of the door. He wonders how much Eldon and Halila have changed now they're fending for themselves in the wider world.

The door swings open and Halila walks in. Question answered: *more than he'd been expecting*.

Her hair's reverted to its natural black, pin-prick scars have replaced some of the more uncomfortable piercings, and a long-sleeved purple shirt hides the tattoos on her arms. But not the SOCIO on the fingers of her right hand and PATH on the left.

The reason for her moderation soon becomes clear.

'Town planning,' she says in response to his enquiry. 'Checking that extension applications conform to the regs.'

Steve nods. 'Mmm, interesting.'

'Fuck off, Steve! It's boring as hell. Boring bloody office full of middle-class guys in white shirts with pens in their top pockets.'

She explains, switching from her usual soft Brummie to a faux RP, that she got the job only when she agreed to alter her appearance "to conform to current client expectations of attire and personal appearance appropriate for a professional local government officer."

Steve smiles. She must have been desperate, he thinks.

'The only interesting person in the whole fucking building,' Halila goes on, 'is a butch bitch who plays rugby at weekends and comes in

Mondays with mud on her knees. Would she let me talk to her? Like fuck! Terrified of the thought police. When I asked her whether her mum was gay, too, she clammed up like a nun's cunt.'

Steve winces. He's forgotten how spicy Halila's talk can be. 'So you're still into that weird stuff, eh?'

Halila snorts. 'Course I am, Steve! You think I'd go through all that family shit and not wanna know where it comes from? It wasn't just, like, your ordinary Bangla macho, as you oughta remember, Steve.'

Of course, but there wasn't much *to* remember. When they were dating, Halila talked a bit about what fuelled her interest in the weird, but she always stopped short of details. He hadn't taken it further. The reticence of someone normally so frank unsettled him. "Whatever it was," he explained to Zoe shortly after they met, "it must've been pretty bad."

The mood lightens when Eldon bounds in. 'Hi guys! Sorry I'm late. Had a bit of stuff to sort out in the office.'

Unsure whether to believe him, Steve and Halila exchange quizzical glances. With the old

Eldon, "a bit of stuff in the office" would have meant only one thing. But now? Suit, tie, clean black shoes, cool haircut, one discrete earring, no visible tattoo… has someone managed to tame him?

It's soon clear that he has been tamed – by himself. The bank of mum and dad dried up when their building business went bust. Eldon's job with Blue Sky Travel was suddenly serious. He arrives on time, leaves late, and in between uses his charm to assure clients that he'll arrange a holiday of a lifetime for them – happiness personally guaranteed by Eldon Bubb. ("And if you're not one hundred percent satisfied, madam, please feel free to come in here when you get back and wipe the smile right off my face!" No one has yet done so.) He plans, checks and double checks far more assiduously than he ever did for a piece of coursework, and it's paying off. Every month he tops the office customer satisfaction chart. There's even talk of him being in line for promotion to branch manager.

Steve and Halila listen with a mix of surprise and admiration. 'I knew you always had it in you, Eldon,' says Steve.

Halila laughs. 'Liar! Come on, Steve, admit it: you're as surprised as me.'

Steve blushes before Eldon's new-found customer courtesy comes to his rescue. 'Doesn't matter, Halila. Enough of me. What about you, Steve? Tell us all about married life.' He grins and glances down at his friend's ankle. 'Left the ball and chain at home, eh?'

Steve tells a happy, normal story, supported by wedding photographs on his phone, of two good, earnest young people starting out together. Eldon and Halila listen politely and make appropriate remarks about the pictures. Is Eldon a little bit jealous? Maybe. But not Halila.

'Good for you, Steve. Glad it's working out. Not my scene, but sounds, like, cool.'

Steve had bought the first round of drinks. Eldon now gets a second. 'Come on then Halila,' he says when he's sitting down again, 'how about you?'

She runs through what she's already told Steve, about her job with local government and how she's continuing her weirdo research in her spare time.

'I admire you,' says Eldon. Halila mouths an obscenity and gives him the finger. 'No, seriously

Halila. You're amazing. You just don't give up, do you?'

'I can't.'

Steve, always literal minded, looks at her quizzically. 'Meaning?'

For the first time since they'd met her, Halila looks sheepish. *My God!* thinks Eldon. *I could almost feel sorry for her.* His ability to empathise has always been part of his charm.

'No point,' says Halila quietly.

'No point in what?' asks Steve.

'No point in telling you. Or anyone.'

Eldon leans forward, stares into his beer for a moment, then asks, 'Got anything to do with them not accepting you for a PhD?'

Halila gives him a sideways look. 'Always were sharper than you made out, weren't you Eldon? Of course it has. Ignorant, narrow-minded bastards.'

Steve doesn't do oblique. He wants the facts, especially after a pint of 5.5%. 'So, what don't they like about you, Halila? Hair? Colour?'

'Don't be a prat, Steve. Even they are not that dumb.' She pauses and looks at Eldon. 'It's my thesis.'

Eldon nods. 'Go on.'

Halila puts her hands together as if praying. She clicks her bottom teeth against her thumbnails. 'I don't like to talk about it much. It's just that I know something, but I don't know how to prove it.'

Eldon makes a gesture with his right hand, asking her to continue.

'Alright. It's about people the tabloids call "evil", like psychopaths, chronic paedophiles, serial murderers and that lot.' She stares at the wall opposite. 'Well, I know something they don't know themselves.'

She pauses and looks hard and Steve and Eldon in turn. Her face is taut and when Steve seems about to say something, she raises a hand to stop him.

'No, let me finish. You see, they can't help it. They're being controlled by something. It's not physical, like gravity or electromagnetism. But it's there – I can *feel* it.'

Steve and Eldon say nothing for a few moments. Then Steve asks, 'It?'

Halila, relieved at having unburdened herself,

is suddenly alive. 'That's the whole point, Steve. I can't tell you exactly what it is, but I've got a pretty good idea. You know when we talk about someone's force of personality?' Steve nods.

'It's a sort of like that. A living force that takes people over …'

'Go on.'

'OK. You know how, when someone falls in love, they're under their lover's spell, think the sun shines out of their arse, and all that crap?'

Steve nods again, though he wouldn't use the word "crap" for the best thing that's ever happened to him.

'It's like that, except swap love for evil, *pure* evil. I could prove it if I got enough subjects to talk to me.'

'What's the problem?' asks Eldon.

'What isn't? They turned me down for social work, counselling and clinical psychology. They won't even let me be a fucking prison visitor. As soon as I even hint at what I know, it's like "piss off, nutter!" I've got this amazing thesis – a bloody no-brainer – but no fucking evidence.'

Eldon's expression screams "sceptical" in block capitals, but his time with Blue Sky has taught him to play the game. The customer is always right. 'Tried the dark web?' he asks. 'Must be loads of criminal sickos on that.'

It's just a casual, throw-away remark, half joking, but it has consequences.

'And risk losing my job and getting a 3 am on the door from the anti-terrorist pigs? Not bloody worth it, Eldon.'

'What about a VPN?' asks Steve. His practicality was one of the reasons Zoe agreed to marry him.

Halila snorts. 'Arm and a bloody leg. Alright for you guys, but town planning's not exactly city trading. Shitty trading more like.' She takes a drink, puts the glass down, and stares into it like it's going to tell her fortune. 'Anyway, they check up on those who've got them, don't they?' Eldon smiles. 'Nope and nope.'

'Meaning?'

'You can get connected for about twenty-five quid a month. And no one checks up on you; too many people use them. Our office, for a start.

Security reasons.'

Halila looks up. 'No bullshit, Eldon?'

In the yellow pub lights her eyes are dark and unblinking. *A bit like a snake's*, thinks Eldon. He looks offended. 'I don't do bullshit anymore, Halila. Check it out. You'll see.'

'He's right,' Steve chips in. 'Worth a try. Then you can see about the Dark Web without MI5 taking you off in a van.'

'How d'you get access?'

'No idea.'

Eldon's turn to chip in. 'Couple of guys at uni managed it – for a laugh. Really freaked them out.'

Halila is now leaning forward slightly. 'Freaked them out how?'

'They didn't want to say. Just that it was "kinky sick".'

'Really, really sick,' adds Steve. 'Paedos, live rape and murder, animal sex …'

'How do you know?' Halila is staring straight at him. 'You been there?'

Steve's embarrassed. 'Don't be daft. Read about it somewhere.' He adds, 'like everyone else' as insurance.

The snake's eyes are flashing from one man to the other, suspicious, eager.

Eldon – the new, clean Eldon – decides it's time to back-pedal. 'Even if you do find out how to get in, Halila, don't go there. Not worth it.'

Steve picks up on the anxious note. It rings true – he knows Halila better than most. 'Eldon's right.

Not worth it. Your weirdos might come from hell, but there's no need to go there to meet them.'

Eldon steers them back onto the main road. 'Too bloody hot, for a start. I'll get another round to cool us down. Come on Halila, there must be something else in your life other than weirdos?

What's your boss like?'

'Total prat. Made a pass at me last week.'

This is Eldon's territory. 'There's a protocol on that sort of thing. We've got it posted behind the doors in all the toilets.'

The subject has changed. Forty-five minutes later, Steve says he has to leave because Zoe's cooking dinner. Halila is also eager to go – she has something to do at home – and the party breaks up. It's been good, and they agree to try and meet up every couple of months. For old time's sake.

'November 21st, same time, same place,' calls Steve as he pulls open the swing door and steps out into the street.

Halila nods. Her eyes are still glittering sightlessly.

Before the November get-together, Eldon and Steve exchange a few messages. The subtext is mildly self-congratulatory: they have successfully moved on to the next stage after uni, like everyone should. They talk of wanting to help Halila, who seems stuck in a nerdy late-teen time warp, and agree to maintain a united front at the next meeting. After all, Halila was their mate once. They'll help her to get real.

The plan fails. Not because Halila won't listen, nor because they don't explain properly. It fails because she beats them to it. When the pub door swings inwards, she swings in too, bouncing, almost dancing, with a toothpaste-advert grin on her face. Hair neat-cut, cool shirt and makeup – yes, makeup: for the first time ever, Halila wears lipstick, eye liner and mascara. The black framing makes her eyes brighter, and a hint of blush gives her a healthy, farm girl look.

The men are bemused, then relieved.

'Hi guys! You ok?' Her voice has changed, too: lighter, almost pre-teen.

Eldon leads the chorus of approval. 'Hey Halila, you look great!'

'Really cool,' agrees Steve.

'Thanks guys. Yeah, things have been a bit better recently. Going well.'

Eldon asks the obvious. 'Come on. Who is it?'

Steve notes the genderless question. Not having experienced Eldon's customer awareness programme, he would probably have said 'he'.

'Just someone.'

'Special?'

'Sort of, yeah.'

'Tight arse!' Steve feels left out. 'Is that all we're going to get?'

'What else d'you want?'

Steve sits back with his hands behind his head. He doesn't want to come over all Gestapo. 'Well, like, someone at work?'

'Of course.'

He searches for the right word. 'Charisma?'

'Yeah. Shit loads.'

She doesn't get more specific and they don't learn the gender, but they've got enough. Halila's going straight, back in their world, a place they understand and approve of. VPNs and the Dark Web are not even mentioned.

When it's clear Halila's not going to reveal any more, it's on to Eldon's office success and how Steve and Zoe are thinking of buying a house.

'Bank of Zoe's parents,' he explains.

Eldon calls him a lucky bastard. He's got at

least another five years of saving before he'll be able to do the same.

'How about you, Halila?'

'Ha fucking ha! *If* I wanted to and *if*, on my money, I saved for 120 years, I might be able to afford a deposit on one the smallest houses in my street.

Steve asks where it is.

'Haberdasher Street, Hoxton. One-bed basement flat.'

Eldon wants to ask whether there's any chance of her going fifty-fifty with whoever he or she is that is responsible for the mascara, but he decides against it. Too risky.

After that, it's Instagram, football and Netflix before reminiscence. Their student days are not long gone, but they're already ancient history and mythology drapes first year discos as thickly as Dunkirk and Thermopylae.

The men do most of the talking. Halila smiles and throws in the occasional word, but mainly she watches. What she's looking at is hard to tell. The next day, in a text, Eldon tells Steve it's what love does to you. He agrees. Good for her.

Halila wears the same faraway expression when the three meet at the end of January. It's her only feature that hasn't changed. She's lost weight, lots of it, and a haunted look hangs on her face like a mask in a Greek tragedy. The makeup is still there but it's smudgy, obviously applied in a hurry, and the vermillion lipstick and pink blusher only highlight the grey pallor of the surrounding skin. The glaze of her eyes is frosted.

If she didn't look so sick, Steve thinks, it might be funny: Halila coming out as a clown.

Eldon, trained to treat every customer as if they were royalty, switches on his smile and asks earnestly how she is. What's he expecting? Illness? Broken heart? Unemployment? All wrong.

'Yeah, great.'

'Really?'

She knows what he's asking and regrets coming.

But now she's here … 'Maybe bit … tired. Lot on.'

'Work ok?'

'Yeah, yeah. Cool.'

Steve is more direct. 'You look a little, well, peaky, Halila. Love life still, like, going strong? He's treating you ok?'

The effect is instantaneous. Her head jerks up and a low-watt glow comes on in her eyes. Her bony fingers grasp the edge of the table.

'That criti … criti-ism? Is it? Then don't!'

'Sorry. Only asking.'

'I said don't! Mind yer own fucking–' She pauses, searching for the word. 'Busi … business.'

'Just trying to help, Halila. We're your friends, and you don't seem …'

When she makes an effort to stand, he leaves the sentence unfinished.

'Seem what?' she says slowly, sitting back down. 'Seem what?' The repetition is born of frustration as she struggles for what follows. 'We're not *seem*. Me and him. We're real. Two in one. Sym … sym …'

'Card?' suggests Steve with an attempt at a smile.

Oh shit! thinks Eldon. When in a hole, Steve … He goes to the bar to get in the first round.

Halila stares at Steve, but not in disbelief. His quip has not registered. 'Two in one,' she repeats. 'Sym-briosis.'

Steve does not correct her. He takes out his phone to see if there's a message from Zoe. There isn't, so he types, *Back in abt 1 hr. Love you, S xx* and flicks through his social accounts. He's tempted to check out NHS 111, too.

Eldon returns with three pints and tries to lighten the mood. Steve responds, but Halila sits like a painted scarecrow in oversized clothes, saying nothing. She leaves her beer untouched.

The men relax into chat about Christmas and the Premier League before the inevitable reminiscence. Eldon tells a story about a student – Olly somebody – who bought a seminar paper online; while he was reading it out, the rest of the class gradually realised the lecturer was mouthing it, word for word.

'Cool way to deal with cheats,' Eldon says. 'Made Olly feel a right prat. We were all shit scared of plagiarism after that.'

'Yea, neat. Subtle's always best. When was it?' 'Must have been near the end of the first year. It was an Option Course on the Cost of Care – I remember because we talked about that psycho who set fire to his girlfriend's house.'

Beside them, a flicker of light comes on in Halila's eyes. 'Oh yeah. I remember. The cops said he killed her then tried to burn the body.'

Eldon frowns slightly and changes the subject. Halila's eyes frost over again. Her outburst and subsequent taciturnity render the mood as flat as her untasted beer. The men avoid looking at her.

After a quick second pint, the men reach for their coats. Neither of them suggests a fourth reunion. To their astonishment, it's left to Halila.

'Do always have to come alo … alone?'

Eldon pauses for a second. 'Er, sure. If you want to bring someone else along, Halila, a partner or whatever, that's fine by me. How about you, Steve?'

'Er, yes. Fine by me too.'

'Good. I'll see if poss … poss …' The men exchange anxious glances.

'Poss-ible.'

When they've fixed a date, Halila nods, rises awkwardly to her feet, and shuffles towards the door. She moves as if her skeleton has no muscle to support it. She's hunched and drags her feet. Her head lolls lightly.

When she's gone, Steve exhales loudly. 'What the fuck?'

Eldon shrugs. 'Don't ask me. Think we should do something?' 'Like what?'

'I dunno. Call a doctor, maybe?'

'And tell them a friend of ours in acting weird, like a bit out of her mind.'

'More like she doesn't have a mind, not all of it, anyway.'

Steve shakes his head. 'A GP will only say they can't do anything without seeing her.'

'True. But we can message her every now and again to check she's ok.'

'Yes. Think we ought to. However weird she is, she was our mate.' Steve puts on his jacket. 'Who the hell does she want to bring with her?'

'Christ knows. But we'll find out, won't we?'

Steve grins. 'If it's poss … poss …'

'Don't! Gives me the creeps.'

'Me too. Sorry. I'll message her tomorrow.'

'Okay. Alternate weeks. I'll start next Monday.'

Green ticks tell that Halila has received the messages. She does not respond.

Nor does she turn up to the March meeting. Steve gets in the drinks and for thirty-five minutes he and Eldon chat with half an eye on the door. They talk of football, but their minds are elsewhere. They're worried, worried by Halila's absence and by the decision they both know they have to make.

Steve comes out with it first. 'Okay, Eldon, do something or forget her and move on?'

'Been through a lot together.'

''That was years ago. But I get what you mean. She was really sick, wasn't she?

'Pretty scary. Not just that she looked like she was half dead, but her *brain* was half dead. Could hardly speak.'

They sit in silence for a moment. 'Back in January she was a different person,' says Steve.

'She'd just met this man – '

'Sure it's a man?'

'She didn't react when I used "he". Wish I knew who he is. Or what he is.'

'And how she met him. You remember what we told her at our first meeting …'

Steve frowns. 'Christ! You don't think she could've gone there?'

'Looking for sickos? Well, you know Halila. Anything's possible.'

They pause for a drink before Eldon continues, 'She's got this theory, hasn't she? About some outside power controlling killers, paedophiles and so on.'

'Sociopathic offenders. Yes, she got into it because of something that happened at home when she was a teenager. An uncle or something. She didn't talk about it much.'

'Don't blame her.'

'Me neither.' Steve takes another drink. 'Obviously affected her a lot. Funny thing is, it didn't make her angry, like it does most people.'

'You mean Me Too and all that?'

'Yes. She didn't buy into that revenge and justice stuff. Her theory is that they can't help it.'

'She says they've been taken over by some sort of weird controlling force outside of themselves.'

'Yeah. A "personal" thing.' Eldon stares across the bar at an overweight man shovelling coins into a fruit machine. 'Like a sort of devil.'

Steve nods. 'They're into that sort of thing where her family come from, Bangladesh. That's probably where she picked it up.'

Eldon articulates both their thoughts. 'No wonder they wouldn't take her on for a PhD. No uni wants some screwed-up woman researching the influence of the Devil on criminal sociopaths. Imagine *The Sun* getting hold of that!'

Steve rolls his eyes upwards and exhales loudly.

'So she carries on her "research" – he suggests the inverted commas with his fingers in the air – 'on her own. Thanks to us, she gets a VPN and finds her way into the Dark Web to look for evidence.'

Eldon sits back limply. 'She's fucking crazy, isn't she?'

'Sadly, I agree. And somewhere in there she comes across this guy. They meet off-line, she falls for him … And God knows what happened next … You saw the state of her.'

'He's killing her, isn't he, Steve?'

'Probably already done so. Whatever, we've got to do something, haven't we?'

'She lives in Hoxton.'

The memory that helped Steve to his First is still sharp. 'Haberdasher Street. We could start there.'

Eldon has brought up Maps on his phone. 'It must be half a mile long, houses on both sides. Could take us a week to find the right one. And I don't fancy knocking on doors asking for a single woman in a basement. More than my job's worth.'

'We need a number. Maybe we could try her work. They'd also tell us whether she's been in or not. How good are you on the phone, Eldon?'

'Try me. It's my job, isn't it?'

'Okay. Call the Hackney town planning office and if she's there, you can ask her straight out. If she's not, then say you've got, er, uni post to forward. You'll think of something.'

'Flattery will get you everywhere, Steve. And when I've got the number ...'

'We go round and try to persuade her to get help. If it's not too late.'

The two men take the Tube to Old Street and meet at the western end of Haberdasher Street at 7 pm the following evening. As Steve predicted, Eldon had no trouble getting hold of the number. *No, sorry, Ms Hossain has not been in for a few weeks ... Forward her post? You can try, but we've written halfa-dozen times and called her number ... Not a squeak ... Alright, probably shouldn't do this, but since you obviously know her quite well ... Number 153, Flat 1. You're welcome.*

The front door of Number 153 is approached up a short flight of steps, with the entrance to the basement through an iron gate on their left. As Eldon is opening it, a smartly dressed man appears at the front door. Is he the owner? Might be. Looking for Halila Hossain. The man points to the basement. 'Down there.'

'Have you seen her recently?' asks Steve.

'Never see her. Keeps herself to herself. Last contact was when she asked if she could pay for the installation of a fibre optic cable.'

'Any visitors?'

The man frowns. 'You cops?'

'No, friends from uni. We need to speak to her. We think she's not very well.'

The man shrugs and points at the stairs to the basement. 'Help yourselves, though she probably won't let you in. She's a bit odd if you ask me. But pays the rent. Takes all sorts.' He walks off without another word.

No light is visible behind the thick curtain hanging across the basement window. Eldon and Steve go down the steps and use the torches on their phones to look for the bell. There isn't one. They exchange glances and Eldon knocks. No reply. He knocks again. Not a sound.

'Try the door,' says Steve.

'Should we? Christ knows what we'll find. Maybe that nutter ...'

'Come on, Eldon. It's why we came, isn't it?'

Steve grasps the handle and turns. To his surprise, the door opens easily, pushing aside a pile of unopened mail, and the two men step inside. They are met by a strange smell. Later, when Steve is describing it to Zoe, he says it reminded him of when he opened his grandma's wardrobe after her death. Old clothes and dust.

All the lights are off, but the glow from a large flatscreen television shows the room is a mess: unmade bed, floor strewn with books and papers, clothes in a heap on a chair, a table buried beneath old cartons, makeup bottles, and a laptop linked to the television by a long HDMI cable.

Halila, wearing only a dressing gown and with her head resting on a cushion, is asleep in an easy chair before the screen.

Suddenly, the screen comes to life. It's Halila, the old Halila, made-up, healthy-looking and full of energy. She looks straight at them, eyes flashing with devilish fire.

'Hi guys! Really glad you've come! Dying to tell someone. Listen, I've fucking gone and done it, haven't I?'

Steve responds instinctively, 'Done what?'

'Proved it, you bloody wally, Steve! I've found what I was looking for. Actually, he found me. Frigging amazing! Who needs a shit-useless PhD when I've got symbi-fucking-osis? You know what? I'm his slave and I love it. I don't give a fucking damn what you think. Can't wait for you to meet …'

The screen goes blank and the voice stops. Eldon, who has pulled out the plug, switches on the light and turns towards the figure in the chair.

'Halila –' He freezes, mouth open, staring. 'Oh Christ …'

Steve moves forward and places a finger on her neck to check her pulse. As he does so, he dislodges her head so that it lolls forward like a ball of paper. Aghast, he puts his hand under her chin to lift it up again. He's shocked by how light it is, just grey skin over an empty skull.

Last Judgement

'What the fuck's going on up there then?'

'Shh! Reg, not so loud.'

'Alright, Ell. So go on, what's it all about?'

Michelle Schofield raised her Gucci shades
and peered at the enormous painting on the wall
in front of her. 'I dunno, Reg. The bloke at the top
looks like God, doesn't he? Beard and all that.'

'Yeah. He's doing okay. Not like them poor
buggers at the bottom. What they done to have
forks shoved up their arses?'

Michelle lowered her shades. 'I told you to get
one of them audio things they were hiring out
when we come in.' She pointed towards a lean
figure in a black cassock arranging chairs to her
right. 'Go and ask that bloke. He'll know.'

'The poofter in a dress?'

'He's a priest, Reg.'

'Course he is. I'm not daft, Ell.'

Reg Schofield, owner and manager of Scofield
and Hammond ("Always on Pole"), Bristol's
largest scaffolding contractor, strode heavily

towards his target. His Nike Airs squeaked on the marble floor.

'Excuse me, sir. What's going on that picture?'

The priest stood over Reg like a giant bird. 'It is the Last Judgement, monsieur.'

'What's that then?'

'On the last day of the world the God judge living people and dead people.'

Reg frowned. 'God's the guy at the top, right, doing his judging?'

'Oui.'

'What's his evidence?'

'The life, monsieur. Your good behaviours and your bad – your sins. He knows them all and He decides your destination – the Heaven or the Hell. That is his judgement.'

Reg nodded. 'Right, got it. Them lot down the bottom, the ones without any clothes on, they're the sinners getting their comeuppance. Fair enough I suppose, if you believe in that sort of thing.' He paused and looked up at the priest's gaunt face. 'Can I ask you a question, monshure?'

Curé Pascal sensed a challenge. 'Oui, of course,' he replied, fixing Reg with his deep-set black eyes.

Unblinking, the eighteen-stone   scaffolder

returned the gaze. A man who has built up a million-pound business is not easily intimidated, even by a disciple of the Almighty.

'Don't get me wrong, monshure, but do you honestly believe all that stuff?' He nodded his head in the direction of the mural. 'Because if you ask me,' he continued without waiting for a reply, 'it's a load of bollocks. Gold-plated bullshit.'

Pascal did not flinch. 'Of course, you are having your opinion, monsieur. It is your liberté. Maybe we do not think today like the man who made this painting, but please, I am begging you, do not mock all his ideas.' The priest extended a long, bony hand and laid it on Reg's shoulder. 'I am not wanting you to go to the wrong destination, my friend.'

Reg looked down at the hand. 'Thanks mate. Appreciate it. I'll give you a call when some devil's sticking a fork up my arse. But right now, my destination is the little place on the other side of the square where they do steak and chips for fifteen euros.'

With that, he turned his back on the priest and squeaked his way back to his wife. 'Come on, Ell! Let's get out of this place. I'm starving.'

The priest's remarks had put Reg in a foul mood and lunch was not a success. He complained about the speed of the service, the toughness of his steak, the waitress' failure to understand him …

When he decided the second bottle of Domaine du Moulin rouge was less good than the first, Michelle had had enough. 'Honestly, Reg, you're an embarrassment, you are. What's got into you? You're like a bear with a sore head after you come out the cathedral. Was it what that priest bloke said?'

'Mind you own fucking business, Ell!' he snapped, spilling red wine on the tablecloth as he refilled his glass. 'What's wrong is this bleeding holiday you've brought me on.'

Here we go, she thought. Like always, it's my fault. Never his.

She'd have walked out years ago if she hadn't been afraid of what he might do to her. And he would have divorced her and shacked up permanently with one of his young secretaries if his wife hadn't known the truth about what happened one Sunday morning, twenty years ago. Since then they had been locked together in a cell of mutual fear.

After working as scaffolders for ten years, Reg Scofield and Charlie Hammond sold their cars, bought an old lorry, stole or borrowed bits of scaffolding and a few clips, and set up Scofield and Hammond, Scaffolders. In many ways it was an ideal partnership. They had contacts in the trade and were both happy to work 6 am to 6 pm, seven days a week. Charlie was the nice guy, mollifying staff who felt hard done by and clients who said they had been overcharged. Reg was the hard man. He bullied workers – physically sometimes – into doing what he wanted, and his threat to "give my London mates a bell" was usually enough to bring disgruntled customers to heel.

When Reg married Michelle, she took over management of the books and brought a certain formality to the firm. She understood VAT and the importance of making contacts with local builders and their families.

Thanks to her business instinct and the men's hard work, seven years after its establishment, Scofield and Hammond was both well-known throughout Bristol, and, for a scaffolding firm, relatively respected.

Then came the big contract.

The Council had approved a scheme for 2,500 new homes on the south-east outskirts of the city. The company that won the contract agreed to use local sub-contractors, and Scofield and Hammond got the scaffolding job. As long as they didn't screw it up, Reg and Charlie would be wealthy men, sharing an estimated profit of at least £250,000.

At that point, before the first brick was laid in the new development, Charlie had his fatal accident.

It was January and one of the firm's jobs was on the run-down Milton estate where gangs of kids roamed the streets at night, chucking stones and, where they could, climbing the scaffolding on building sites to light fires on the wooden boards. A thirteen-year-old boy had recently died when he fell off, and the Council had ordered all scaffolders to check the security of their frames regularly at weekends when there were no workmen. The two bosses split the job between them, Reg taking Saturdays and Charlie Sundays. They each did a morning and evening check.

Reg did Saturday as usual, returning home about 6 pm after a final look around. The following morning, he left the house while it was still dark and came back a couple of hours later. When Michelle asked him where he'd been, he said he'd been out for a drive to get petrol. She knew instinctively that he was lying but didn't take the matter further. Probably another stupid girl, she told herself.

Only when the police came round later that morning did it dawn on Tracy where Reg had been. A dog walker on the Milton estate had found the body of Charlie Hammond lying on a concrete path beside a block of flats that was encased in Scofield and Hammond scaffolding. Initial reports suggested he had died of multiple injuries after falling from a considerable height. Reg, visibly shocked, told the police that Charlie would have been on site that morning around 8 am to check for overnight interference. As they all knew, there had been a lot of trouble with kids recently …

Reg accompanied the police on their inspection of the site. He had personally checked it the previous evening, he told them, and found it safe and secure. Yes, it had rained all night and the boards were slippery, but Charlie had worked on scaffolding all his life and knew how to look after himself. He could only have fallen if one of the guard rails ... Hang on! Yeah, exactly above where Charlie had fallen, someone had taken the guard rail right off and chucked it down to ground. There it was, sticking in the grass beside the path.

Those bloody kids!

But the kids denied everything, and in the end the coroner declared Charlie's death a tragic accident. There were rumours, of course. One of the Schofield's elderly neighbours thought she had heard Reg's car early that Sunday morning, but she couldn't be sure.

The men working on the Milton site muttered amongst themselves, too: they knew how difficult it would be for someone who didn't know what they were doing to unbolt both ends of a guard rail in the dark. Kids? Never. None of them said anything, however. They didn't trust the police any more than did the residents of Milton estate; besides, they had their jobs to think about. The gaffer had a reputation for sacking shirkers and troublemakers at an hour's notice. No, you didn't mess with Reg Schofield. And no one could prove anything, could they?

Except Michelle. When Reg left the house with the police on the morning of Charlie's death, he had been wearing a clean tracksuit beneath a donkey jacket. She looked for the clothes he had worn when he went out earlier. His waxed jacket, soaking wet, was not on its usual peg in the hall but hanging in the garage. One of the pockets had been partly ripped off, as if someone had grabbed hold of it to stop themselves from … Michelle shivered. If her husband had gone to meet some girl, he would have worn something smart, wouldn't he? But it was his work clothes that had been stuffed into the washing machine. The trousers, like the jacket, were soaking wet. So were his work boots.

Michelle took the jacket and hung it up in its usual place in the hall with the ripped pocket facing outwards. She was standing beside it when Reg returned after the site inspection with the police.

'Bloody aida, Ell,' he said as he came through the door. 'Poor old Charlie!'

When she made no reply, his eyes moved to the jacket. 'Congratulations, Reg,' she said quietly.

'Eh? What you on about?'

'You just made yourself a cool £125,000. Not bad for a morning's work, eh?'

He stepped forward until he was staring

straight into her face. She was sure he was going to hit her – it wouldn't have been the first time. Instead, he said quietly, 'Luckily, bitch, I didn't hear that. If I had, I'd have killed you. Got it?'

She didn't flinch. 'Yes, Reg, I've got it. And now it's just you and me in the business, we'll have to make a real success of it, won't we? Barring accidents, of course.'

It took a moment for her words to sink in. When they did, he grinned. 'That's my Ell, eh? A real success, yeah.'

And it was. Half of the profits from the big deal they spent on themselves; the other half they ploughed back into the firm. Rivals were bought up or forced out of business. The tactics were not always legit, but they worked. Within ten years there was hardly a site in the whole of Bristol without a Schofield and Hammond sign hanging on it somewhere. And when asked by the media or business groups to explain his success, Reg always gave the same answer: 'Hard bloody work, mate. You don't get where I've got by accident.'

The trappings of financial success were predictable. First the large house with a Mercedes on the drive, then the indoor pool, and latterly, following Michelle's quest for sophistication, swapping the summer fortnight on the Costa del Sol for three weeks in a villa near Toulouse in southwest France. Hence the visit to Albi Cathedral and Reg's uncomfortable meeting with Curé Pascal.

Three weeks after their return to England, Reg had a second uncomfortable meeting. Feeling dizzy after climbing fifty feet to inspect the work of a new crew he'd taken on, he went to see his GP to find out if there was anything wrong. He was weighed, measured, and asked questions about his lifestyle and family history. The conclusion was alarming but hardly surprising.

'I'm afraid you've allowed yourself to become obese,' said the earnest young doctor.

'You saying I'm fat?' Reg retorted.

The doctor looked down at her screen. 'It's not so much me saying anything as the statistics, Mr Schofield. I'm simply the messenger. What you choose to do with the message is entirely up to you.'

'What message?'

'Well, unless you alter your lifestyle and manage to lose at least four stone – preferably five

– you are highly likely to develop diabetes and other serious illnesses before the age of sixty. At present, your chances of having a heart attack or stroke within the next ten years are …' she paused to tap quickly at her keyboard … 'somewhere between four- and five-to-one. Those are not good odds, Mr Schofield.'

Confronted by his own mortality for the first time in his life, Reg was curiously deflated. To begin with, he was reluctant to tell Michelle the news – it would be an admission of weakness. When he finally did confess, she almost felt sorry for him. How are the mighty fallen, she thought tactlessly.

Nevertheless, she cooked him healthy meals, converted the snooker room into a gym equipped with top-of-the-range exercise machines, and bought him drawers full of snazzy sportswear. None of it did any good. His weight hovered obstinately between eighteen and nineteen stone, and shortness of breath forced him to give up climbing ladders to inspect work. Then, sitting before the TV one evening with a six pack of Leffe Blond beside him, he happened upon a programme about a man who turned his life around by taking up hiking. The rolling countryside, the wind in your face, the stunning views … Reg was inspired.

'You know, Ell, I could do with a bit of that. Getting away from it all. Bloody sight more fun than peddling me arse off on a fucking exercise bike.'

Michelle was quite taken with the idea, too, and they agreed to make a start on the Brecon Beacons at the weekend. He took his platinum credit card to a specialist outdoor clothing store and, advised by an eager young man with a windswept face and a red beard, kitted himself out with the best hiking gear on the market.

As he was paying, the manager appeared, gave a nod of welcome and asked whether everything was to Reg's satisfaction.

Reg, who had been focussing on entering his pin, looked up in surprise. The voice sounded vaguely familiar – not the accent, which had a Bristol burr to it, but the self-assured, almost condescending delivery. Reg found himself looking up at a very tall, gaunt man in a charcoal suit. His blue-back eyes, the colour of crows, gazed down on him from a thin, pale face.

'Haven't I seen you before somewhere?' Reg

asked, frowning.

'I don't think so, sir. I don't recall seeing you in the shop and I don't go out much when not at work.'

'Strange. Maybe I'm wrong.'

'Maybe, sir.' The manager held out a green and brown card. 'Did young Dickson show you our new Journey's Destination app, sir?'

'No.' Reg looked around; the assistant who had served him was nowhere to be seen. 'Tell us about it, then.'

It was, the manager explained, an invaluable hikers' app developed exclusively for their chain of stores. All one had to do was download it to a phone, log in with the unique code provided with purchase of the card, and the app would become your personal guide to wherever you wished to go. It not only offered a choice of routes – beginner, experienced, professional – but also provided an up-to-date weather forecast and information about interesting features beside the path. For only £24.99, no hiker could afford to set out without one.

Reg was convinced, and the manager dropped the card bearing the app's unique code into the bag with all the other purchases.

'Have it on us, sir,' he said, gently pushing aside Reg's proffered credit card. 'We don't get many customers like yourself. Please accept it as a little gift to welcome you to the world of hiking.' Almost without Reg noticing, he laid a bony hand gently on his shoulder. 'I'm sure you'll find your destination with no trouble at all. Goodbye, sir.'

Cheeky bugger! thought Reg as he left the shop. *Fucking poofters everywhere nowadays!*

When he showed Michelle what he'd bought and told her about the app, she changed her mind about accompanying him at the weekend.

'Why's that, Ell?' he asked, more out of interest than concern. He was quite looking forward to being out in the open on his own. It'd be a chance to blow away a few old cobwebs once and for all.

'Oh, I dunno. Reckon with you out of the way I can get a bit done around the house. You go and do your destination thing. With me there we'd only argue about where to go.'

And so, early on Saturday morning, Reg packed a few things into the car and set out for the Brecon Beacons National Park. He did not return.

Around noon the following day, a party

of walkers found his body at the foot of an escarpment on Pen y Fan, the Park's highest peak. His multiple injuries were commensurate with a fall of several hundred feet. At the end of a short inquest, Avon Coroner Frances Latter declared the death of Reginald Schofield to have been the result of an "unfortunate accident", the deceased having "fallen from a considerable height while walking alone in the Brecon Beacons."

Delivering her verdict, Ms Latter noted two small matters that remained unclear. The first was why someone as inexperienced and unfit as Mr Schofield should have tackled the notoriously treacherous Pen y Fan on his first hike. The second concerned his phone. Not only had it survived the fall intact, but the deceased had somehow managed to keep hold of it during his fall. The unfortunate young woman who was first to reach the body burst into tears when she read the message still showing on the screen: "You Have Reached Your Destination."

Soon afterwards, the battery died. When Michelle recharged it to see the message for herself, she found the Journey's Destination app had been deleted. She enquired in the shop where Reg had bought the activation code. The young man who had served him was very sorry to hear of the tragic accident. He was, however, unable to help further. No, the store had never sold activation codes for an app called Journey's Destination – in fact, neither he nor any of his outdoor friends had ever heard of it. Nor had the store manager, a short, rather chubby young man with fair hair.

About the Author

Prizewinning author Stewart Ross taught at all levels in the UK, the USA, the Middle East and Sri Lanka before becoming a full-time writer in 1989. He has published many works of fiction and nonfiction, including over 50 novels for adults and for children. He has also written plays, lyrics and poetry, and his books have been translated into some 20 languages. When not working in a large hut in the garden, Stewart visits schools, colleges and universities in the UK, France and elsewhere to talk about writing and pass on his passion for words.

Find out more on *stewartross.com*

Printed in Great Britain
by Amazon

22739740R00118